Silent Night, Deadly Night

RICHARD L. MABRY, M.D.

ISBN-13: 9781518641091

Books by Richard L. Mabry, MD

Novels of Medical Suspense
:

Code Blue
Medical Error
Diagnosis Death
Lethal Remedy
Stress Test
Heart Failure
Critical Condition
Fatal Trauma
Miracle Drug

Novellas

Rx Murder

Nonfiction

The Tender Scar: Life After The Death Of A Spouse

WHAT OTHERS SAY ABOUT RICHARD MABRY'S BOOKS

(about *Miracle Drug*)
"Excellent story. Excellently crafted. Great characters. Great plot."

DiAnn Mills, Christy Award winning author of *Deadlock*

(about *Fatal Trauma*)
"Fatal Trauma asks big questions of faith, priorities, and meaning all within the context of a tightly crafted medical drama."

-Steven James, best-selling
author of Placebo and Checkmate

(about *Critical Condition*)
"A rousing pace, an intricately crafted plot and a subtle hint of romance draw the reader in. Mabry has the uncommon ability to take medical details and make them understandable, while still maintaining accuracy and intrigue. He will leave you asking whodunit until the end."

Romantic Times Book Reviews (4 ½ stars)

(about *Heart Failure*)
"You are not going to want to miss Dr. Richard Mabry's newest thrill ride! Mabry combines his medical expertise with a story that will keep you on the edge of your seat."

USA Today

(about *Stress Test*)
"Original and profound. I found the Christian message engaging and fascinating, and the story a thrill-a-minute."

Michael Palmer, NYT best-selling author of *Oath Of Office*

(about *Lethal Remedy*)
"Richard, a doctor himself, knows our greatest fears, and he knows the value life. His thrillers balance the thrills with great heart and the loving relationships that make us most human."

—*The Big Thrill* (International Thriller Writers)

(about *Diagnosis Death*)
"...Another riveting medical drama, the third in his Prescription for Trouble series. Full of sudden twists and turns, the novel's fast pace makes it hard to put down." (4 ½ stars)

~*Romantic Times Book Reviews*

(about *Medical Error*)
"Richard Mabry's *Medical Error* kept me guessing even as I eagerly turned the pages to see what would happen next. If you like medical suspense, this one will keep you glued to your favorite reading chair!"

~Angela Hunt, author of *When Darkness Comes*.

(about *Code Blue*)
"Rarely does a debut novel draw me in and rivet my attention as Dr. Richard Mabry's *Code Blue* did.. I'm already looking forward to Dr. Mabry's next release."

-BJ Hoff, author of The Emerald Ballad series and The Riverhaven Years.

1

It was a scene that made you want to sing "Silent Night"—or at least hum a few bars. A full moon shone on the blanket of snow covering the yard of the home. Drapes at each side of a picture window were drawn back to display the holiday decorations within. Although Christmas had come and gone five days earlier, the tree's colored lights still burned, reflecting off the ornaments and tinsel scattered through the branches. Holiday lights on the eaves of the house at Redman Lane cast a multicolored glow over the scene.

The only false note was the front door of the house, standing wide open and spilling light onto a narrow path across the porch.

Officer Adela Reyes of the Hilton Police Department slowed her cruiser to a stop at the curb. An open door at three in the morning indicated either trouble or a careless homeowner. She scanned the scene before lifting the microphone from its clip on her patrol car's dashboard. Reyes pressed the button to transmit. "This is Officer Reyes. I've got an open front door and lights still on at 7710 Redman Lane. I'm going to check it out."

"Roger. Are you requesting backup?"

"I don't think so. It's probably just someone who forgot to lock up. I'll call in if I need help."

She flipped on the car's strobes to warn anyone coming up on her cruiser, although she doubted there'd be any traffic on this residential street at this time of night—or rather, of morning. With one hand on her holstered Glock, a five-cell flashlight in her other hand—both for illumination and to use as a club—she carefully approached the house, slogging through the undisturbed snow of the front yard.

When she reached the front porch, Reyes knocked loudly on the frame of the open door. "Police. Anyone home?" She repeated this several times before she walked inside. She'd learned that houses give off vibes when they were occupied, and her gut told her this one was empty. Nevertheless, she went through each room, calling out, scanning every hiding place. When she had satisfied herself that the house was unoccupied, she keyed the microphone secured to the epaulet near the collar of her uniform.

"This is Reyes again. That house with the open door seems unoccupied." She paused to think about her course of action. "I'll push the button to lock the door when I leave."

After shutting the door, she walked back to her squad car, when she noticed a peculiar mound of snow off to one side of the path. The little hill was about three feet by six, roughly the same dimensions as a grave. There was nothing unusual about snow piling up in mounds and drifts, but this one looked different somehow. Reyes was curious about what might be under that mound. Was it a toy of some sort, left in the yard and covered with snow? She decided to give it a look. As she approached, she held the flashlight in her left hand, while her right hovered near her holstered weapon.

Reyes edged over and kicked a bit of snow away from the mound with a booted foot. She aimed her flashlight downward to see what she'd exposed, then stepped back and gave an almost silent gasp. Up from the hole she'd made in the snow stared a pair of eyes—eyes in the face of a dead woman.

Two marked police cars stood in front of the house, their strobes still flashing and spreading alternating patterns of red and blue onto the white blanket of snow that covered the yard. Another dark sedan was parked nearby, the red lights behind the grill glowing more softly. A silver Land Rover and an ambulance completed the array of vehicles parked helter-skelter in front of the house.

A portable generator powered lights that were aimed at the area. Reyes secured the last of the yellow crime scene tape that formed a barrier around the frozen corpse. She stepped back out of the way as Patsy Sawyer, her badge and ID hanging around her neck, meticulously recorded every detail of the scene with her video camera.

When Patsy was finished, she turned to an older man who stood patiently behind the yellow tape, his breath coming in small clouds of condensation. "Doc, she's all yours."

The pathologist removed his gloved hands from the pockets of his overcoat and approached the body. "Want to give me a hand here?" he called to Reyes.

"Yes sir?"

"Get the trenching tool out of your patrol car. You need to move this snow away and completely expose the woman so I can have a look."

He didn't offer to help her, and she didn't expect him to. Working carefully, Reyes scooped the snow away until the body was uncovered. The corpse was that of an elderly woman. Her eyes were open, and her face bore an expression of surprise. She was laid out as straight as a soldier at attention, staring upward into eternity.

The doctor knelt at the side of the dead woman. He removed his gloves and placed his fingertips on her neck. After a few moments, he turned to where Reyes was standing with another officer and said, "You already know she's dead. I'll make it official. You need anything more from me?"

Sergeant Jason Fuller, the uniformed man next to Reyes, answered. "Not right now. Thanks, Doc."

"I'll know more after we do the autopsy," the doctor said. "Because the body is essentially frozen, determination of the time of death will depend on what you learn from the people you interview. Ready for me to have the attendants take the body away?"

The sergeant held up a hand. "Give me a minute." He turned to the crime scene tech. "Patsy, do you need to get some more video now that the body is uncovered?"

"I shot some while Officer Reyes was removing the snow. Let me get just a bit more, though."

When that was done, Fuller squatted and carefully surveyed the scene from a lower viewpoint. He nodded, slowly rose, and took a few steps forward, carefully placing his feet in the footprints already made by others.

When he reached the corpse, he looked down at the woman's body, frowning occasionally, saying nothing. Finally Sergeant Fuller said, "Okay, Doc. The attendants can bag her. Give me a call when you know more."

Fuller turned to Reyes. "What did you see?"

She forced herself to watch as the attendants maneuvered the frozen corpse into a body bag and loaded it onto a stretcher. "The deceased is an elderly Caucasian female wearing what women of her age call, I believe, a housecoat. No external signs of trauma. No blood. And when I found her, she was lying here under a mound of snow in freezing weather."

"So what happened?" Fuller asked.

"She went out in the yard for some reason. She must have had a stroke or heart attack and died rather suddenly." Reyes looked at the sky. "We've had snow off and on for several days. It started to snow heavily a few hours ago—it covered her tracks and, eventually, her body."

"Your first dead body?" he asked.

"No sir. Just the first one I've seen outside a coffin," she said. "I guess you've seen lots of them."

The ambulance doors slammed, and the vehicle drove slowly away. No flashing lights or blaring siren. There was no hurry involved in the woman's final journey.

Fuller removed his billed police cap and ran his hand through his unruly gray hair. He reached under his heavy uniform coat and tugged at his belt, moving his holstered pistol to ride more comfortably on his hip. "Yeah, in thirty years on the Dallas police force, I saw my share of dead bodies." He looked away for a moment. "I figured when I retired here to Hilton, I'd never take part in another murder investigation, but I guess I was wrong."

"Why?" Reyes asked. "You think she was murdered? Don't you agree with the scenario I described?"

Fuller shook his head. "I'm not convinced."

"What's wrong with the way I laid it out?" Reyes asked.

"To begin with, why did she come outside in the middle of the night?" he asked.

"Maybe she heard a noise. She might have been confused and started looking for the newspaper." Reyes shrugged. "We may never know the reason."

"How come she's lying on her back? Don't most people fall facedown—crumple a bit? But she's supine, straight as a board, as though she'd been laid out."

"I . . . I can't explain that, sir."

"Why didn't anyone see her?"

Reyes pushed back the cuff of her uniform coat and checked the time. "It's after three in the morning. As I said, the snow probably covered her pretty quickly. There's nobody out at this time of the morning. The newspaper won't be delivered for another couple of hours. If I hadn't stopped my patrol car because of the open door, she might have lain under that mound of snow until everything melted."

"I don't think that's how it happened," Fuller said.

"How can you be sure?"

"I won't be one-hundred-percent certain until after the autopsy, but I don't think this was an accident."

"Do you see something I've missed?" Reyes asked. "Other than what you've already mentioned?"

"When you saw those bodies in their caskets, what kind of shoes were they wearing?"

"I . . . I don't really know. I never noticed."

"That's because they don't put shoes on bodies laid out for burial. The casket covers the lower half of the corpses." He pointed. "Now, think about what you saw, and tell me what else doesn't jibe with your story of a woman going out in the yard, falling because of a stroke or heart attack, and freezing to death."

Reyes looked, and suddenly the sergeant's point was clear to her. This wasn't an accidental death. This was probably a homicide—of a woman whose frozen corpse had bare feet.

2

Dr. Laura Morris shivered despite the heavy coat she wore. It was rare for her to go out at night to see a patient, but the call from the emergency room worried her. One of her patients, Sara Webb, had been brought in around midnight after suffering her first grand mal seizure. The ER doctor had called Laura to ask about medications the woman might be taking.

"She's not on any meds from me that would explain this," Laura said. "Go ahead with your work-up. I think I'll come out and have a look at her."

Despite the snow that was falling, the major streets were passable, and Laura's Chevrolet Malibu didn't skid even one time on the way to the emergency room. Once she was there, she talked briefly to Sara's family before reviewing the CT of her patient's head that the emergency room physician had ordered. The two doctors agreed—the woman likely had a tumor pressing on her brain.

Sara was still obtunded from her seizure and the medication given her afterward, so Laura talked with the woman's family. "The scan of her head showed a tumor on her brain, probably what's called a meningioma. Many of these are benign, but either way, surgical intervention is called for. The neurosurgeon I have in mind is very good. I think you'll like him, and he'll take good care of Sara."

Once she'd made the handoff to the specialist, Laura headed for the staff parking lot. Whether it was because of the holidays, the late hour, or the weather, there were only a few cars in the staff lot. When they were first married, her husband, a surgeon, had suggested that Laura carry a pistol when she went out at night. "You need to protect yourself," Carter said. "If not a gun, then at least carry a Taser, or a canister of Mace."

"No. I'll be fine," Laura had said. And generally she'd felt safe, even in circumstances and locations that others might fear. But, for some reason, tonight it was different. She felt a tingling between her shoulder blades, and found herself looking over her shoulder frequently.

She was almost to her car, when a vehicle near hers roared into life. The lights came on, almost blinding her, and the car—a dark sedan—headed straight for her. Laura hesitated for only a second or so before jumping behind a Range Rover parked nearby. The dark sedan barely clipped the front bumper of the large SUV before roaring off into the darkness.

Laura couldn't believe someone tried to run over her. When the full realization of what just happened started to hit her, her heart hammered in her chest. Beads of perspiration rolled down between her shoulder blades despite the cold outside temperature. She stood there, leaning on the fender of the vehicle where she'd taken shelter, waiting for her adrenaline level to drop to more normal levels.

She looked around her, but no one seemed to be responding to the episode in the parking lot. Once Laura felt less shaken and more in control, she eased toward her car, using the vehicles parked nearby for cover. When she was inside her Chevy, she locked all the doors, started the engine, and drove cautiously home.

She intended to relate the experience to her husband when she got home, but two things stopped her. The first was that she realized he'd probably use this to resurrect his argument that she should carry a gun when going out at night. The second was that he appeared to be sound asleep when she tiptoed into the bedroom.

The next morning, Laura decided to downplay the episode. "I think someone just had too much Christmas cheer to drink," she told her husband, Dr. Carter Hawkins.

"So you're still not going to carry—"

"No. I don't like guns, and don't want one around."

She was finishing her breakfast, when the phone in the front room rang. As she hurried to answer it, Carter passed her in the hall, a travel cup of coffee in his hand. "Got to hurry. I need to see a couple of post-ops before my first case." He brushed her cheek with a kiss before heading for the door to the garage.

Laura shook her head. *Just like a surgeon—always in a hurry.* She picked up the phone right before the call rolled over to voice mail.

After the usual explanation that, yes, she was Dr. Morris, although her husband's name was Dr. Hawkins, the man on the other end of the phone said, "Doctor, this is Sergeant Fuller of the Hilton Police. Sorry to call so early."

"I was already up," Laura said. "How can I help you?"

"Ma'am, I mainly wanted to see if you were at home. I need to come by to talk with you in person. Would half an hour be too soon?"

Why would the police call her? Had something happened to her family? She and her husband had no children. Her parents were dead. "Look, Sergeant. I'm a physician. I don't think you can give me any news I can't handle. In half an hour, I want to be on my way to the hospital to make rounds."

She heard Fuller sigh. "Okay, we'll do it your way. Is Ina Bell Patrick your aunt?"

"Yes," Laura said. "She's my late mother's only sister. Has something happened to Aunt Ina?"

"Yes ma'am," Fuller said. "I'm afraid it has."

Laura listened as Fuller told her of the grisly finding Patrolman Reyes had made a few hours ago. "Your aunt's body is being transported to Fort Worth, where the medical examiner will perform an autopsy."

Poor Aunt Ina. Laura was glad she and Carter had been there to help the woman celebrate Christmas. Then she realized it would be up to her to make the final arrangements. Aunt Ina had no one else—no husband, no children, no siblings.

"Doctor Morris?"

"I'm sorry," she said. "I got sidetracked in my thinking. Would you repeat that?"

"Yes ma'am. When can you come by police headquarters?"

"Do you need for me to go to the mortuary and make some sort of identification?"

"No ma'am. Your aunt's purse was on a table in the living room of her house. It contained an expired driver's license with her picture, and we were able to make an identification from that and some other papers we found. But I do need to ask you a few questions."

"What kind of questions?" Laura had a disturbing thought. "Will I need an attorney?"

"That's up to you," the policeman said. "You see, we think it's likely your aunt was murdered."

It took a minute for Laura to process that last statement. Murder? That happened in other families. Not in hers.

She had lots of questions, but the sergeant told her he'd answer them all when she came down to the police station. After she hung up, Laura wondered whom she should call first with this news. Carter? No, he needed to concentrate on his surgery. She'd call him later. Robert? Yes she should notify him. What about Zack? No. There was no way to reach her brother. There hadn't been for almost five years.

Their parents had died in a taxi crash as they headed to a cruise ship to celebrate the start of their retirement. It had shocked all three of the children—Laura, Robert, and Zack—but they each dealt with it in different ways.

Laura, always the sensible one, mourned while she made the arrangements for her parents' service, the same way she was sure she would for her aunt. A week after the tragedy, Robert was absorbed once more in his law practice, and showed no external evidence of grief. Zack, who was single, kept to himself, staying in their parents' home until the estate was settled. Shortly thereafter, he'd showed up on Laura's doorstep to tell her he was leaving town.

"Where are you going?" she'd asked him. "How will we get in touch with you?"

"I don't know where I'm going," Zack said. "Right now, I just want to get out of Hilton. And this is my chance." He gave her a brotherly kiss. "I'll drop you a line soon."

But he hadn't. Laura continued to pray for her younger brother, but those prayers came less frequently as months turned to years with no word from him. And now, here he was, back in her thoughts again.

Reyes sat in the squad room and listened as Sergeant Fuller talked with Ms. Patrick's niece. When he'd ended the call, Fuller looked at her and said, "Aren't you supposed to be off duty by now?"

"Yes. But I wanted to stick around and listen while you talked with the woman's next of kin. I think I can learn from you."

"How long have you been an officer in this department?" Fuller asked.

"A little less than a year, sir. I joined right after graduating from college with my degree in criminal justice. I figured working in a smaller department like this one would give me a better chance for advancement than I'd get in one of the larger forces."

What Reyes didn't say was that, about the time she joined the Hilton Police Department, she discovered there was really no slot for a full-time detective. Instead, Sergeant Fuller, because of his experience, acted as head of the Criminal Investigation Team for any major crimes. He generally chose one of the senior officers to work with him. She wanted to get in her bid before he made that choice.

She took a deep breath and plunged in. "I want to work with you on this case," she said.

"And why do you think I should choose you?" Fuller asked.

"This started out as my case," Reyes said. "I've been with you on it so far. I may be a rookie, but I'm a quick learner and I work hard." She ran her tongue over lips that had suddenly gone dry. "If you give me this chance, you won't regret it."

Fuller leaned back in his desk chair and stared at the ceiling. "So you really want in on this."

"Yes sir."

"Okay. If we're going to be working together, lose the 'sir.' I'm 'Sergeant' or 'Sergeant Fuller.' Got that?"

"Yes . . . Yes, Sergeant."

"I'll tell the chief you're temporarily assigned to this case with me. Now, what I intend to do next is interview some people. You sit in, take notes, and keep your mouth shut unless I ask you a question. Clear?"

"Clear," Reyes said.

"Hey, Adela."

Reyes turned when she heard a familiar voice call her name. She looked up to see Officer Terry Briggs, standing near where she sat. He lowered his voice. "Still around?" Briggs said. "I thought your tour was over."

"I'm working a possible homicide with Sergeant Fuller." She nodded to indicate the sergeant. He was bent over documents at his desk, but there was no doubt in her mind that he had his ears open.

"Oh," Briggs said.

He took off his cap and ran his hand through his red hair. His complexion was fair, not dark, but it had not escaped Reyes that he was definitely tall and handsome. "Well, I just saw you here and thought I'd say hello," he said.

"What are you doing back at the station right now?" she asked.

"Brought in a guy I tagged for DUI. I guess it's time to get back on patrol, though." He looked for a moment at Fuller, still sitting nearby. "If you . . ." He shook his head. "Never mind. I'll catch you another time."

After Briggs left, Fuller looked up at Reyes. "You and Officer Briggs seem pretty friendly."

"I've seen him around," she said. "That's all."

"Well, it would appear he's got more than a passing interest in you," Fuller said. "But right now, why don't we do something about solving this case?"

"Shouldn't you be going?" Claudia Morris asked her husband.

"I'm leaving right now," Robert Morris replied. His gray pinstripe suit, freshly cleaned and pressed, hung on him just as the tailor planned. The French cuffs of his crisp white shirt were held closed by onyx cuff links. His perfectly knotted red-figured tie matched the display handkerchief showing in the breast pocket of the suit coat. And his wingtip, lace-up Italian-made shoes were shined to just the right luster.

Robert was headed for court, but not as a defendant. He would give his final arguments today in an important civil case. One of the first things he'd learned in law school was that he didn't want to practice criminal law. Instead, he'd concentrated on the specialized field of oil-and-gas law. He was very good at it and didn't mind letting people know that.

He picked up his Halliburton briefcase, gave his wife a perfunctory kiss on the cheek, and was on his way out, when he heard the phone inside his house ring. *Who could be calling this early?* Well, whoever it was, Claudia could handle it. The judge was very strict about punctuality in his courtroom.

Robert walked through the kitchen and into the garage of his luxury home in one of the nicer suburbs of Fort Worth. He pushed the button to raise the garage door, and shivered at the gusts of chilly wind that blew in. He climbed into his car and started the engine to let it get warm.

He was pleased to see that the young man he'd hired yesterday to clean the snow from his driveway had done so early this morning, after the flurries ceased. Not only that, the city had plowed the streets so Robert should be able to drive to the courthouse with no problem. Things were looking up. He put his silver BMW into Reverse and was halfway out the driveway, when Claudia hurried through the front door of the house, clutching her coat around her. He stopped and rolled down his car window.

"Robert, Laura just called," she said, her breath making little puffs of condensation in the cold air. "She needs to talk with you."

He frowned at this news. A glance at the Rolex on his wrist told him he had to be on his way. "I'll call her from the car," Robert said. "Now I've got to go."

Once he was underway, he instructed his phone, via the Bluetooth setup of the car, to "Call Laura."

In a moment, his younger sister answered. "Robert," she said without preamble, "our Aunt Ina has died."

"I'm sorry to hear that," he said. He tried to call up any sentimental memories of his late mother's only sister, but failed. He had memories, but they were more practical than sentimental. He wondered if she'd left . . . Never mind. "Are you making the arrangements for a memorial service? If you want me to pay half the cost of a family spray for the casket, I'll be glad to go in with you. Just let me know—"

"Stop!" Laura said. "This isn't about final arrangements." She paused. "A policeman called to give me the news, and he wants to question me."

"Why?" Robert asked.

"He said he doesn't think Aunt Ina's death was natural. She may have been murdered."

"Why would they think that?" Robert squinted into the sun as he made the turn toward the courthouse. "Never mind. Do you want me to recommend a lawyer to go with you when you talk with the policeman? I don't do criminal law, but I know a couple of lawyers who do."

"I can take care of that if I need one," Laura said. "But if I were you, I'd expect the police to be contacting you shortly—asking where you were last night."

Robert wheeled into a parking place but kept the motor running. He wanted to wind up this conversation before he left the car. "Why would they want my alibi for the time she died?"

"If someone murdered Aunt Ina, who inherits her money? She and Uncle Bill didn't have any children. Unless I'm very wrong, you and I—and Zack, if he can be found—are the ones who get it."

"Well, I don't have time for this right now," he said. "I'll call you later. Right now, I have to get ready to wind up this trial."

As he parked his car, Robert couldn't help thinking about Aunt Ina's money. Had she finally written a will after his talk with her? If she'd cut out Zack, that meant he'd get half of what she left behind, not a third. He didn't know the exact value of her estate, but her husband had owned a pretty successful insurance firm, probably had a large policy or two on himself. Robert figured he'd left her well fixed.

If she'd made a will, why hadn't she taken him up on his offer to have one of his colleagues draw one for her free of charge? And if there was one, even a will he hadn't drafted, would she have a copy at her house? That would take some looking into.

He didn't want to count those chickens before they hatched, but he couldn't help thinking what more money could mean for him and Claudia. They could certainly use it. He smiled as he made his way into the courthouse.

When Laura ended the call with Sergeant Fuller, she thought about calling her husband to let him know what was going on. Then again, he was preparing for a surgical case, and she hated to distract him. She decided to wait until his usual noontime call. There'd be plenty of time then.

Laura was a bit late getting to the office that morning. Since she didn't want rumors to start floating around the clinic where she worked, she called her nurse, Courtney, into her office. "My Aunt Ina died last night," Laura said. "I may be getting a call from the police this morning."

"I'm sorry to hear about your loss. But why would the police call?"

"That's why I wanted to tell you before rumors start flying. The detective who talked with me this morning seemed to think her death wasn't from natural causes." The look Courtney gave her indicated the nurse had more questions, and Laura figured one of them was "Do they suspect you?"

However, all Courtney said was, "Do we need to cancel any patient appointments?" She looked at the appointment list before she handed it to Laura. "I'm sure one of the other FPs would cover for you."

"I don't think that'll be necessary," Laura said. "This is my scheduled afternoon off, so I'll go by the police station when I finish here. And, as I recall, we're going to close early tomorrow for New Year's Eve."

"We're going to try," Courtney said. "But I'll make sure you get out of here by noon. Again, I'm sorry to hear about your aunt."

Laura scanned the phone messages on her desk, decided there was nothing there that couldn't wait until her first break, and said, "Is my first patient ready?"

"Waiting for you in Room One," was all Courtney said, but her facial expression told Laura a lot more than that. "It's Mrs. Sanderson."

It hadn't taken long for Laura to discover that every practice had its patients like Mrs. Sanderson. But just because a person could be a pain didn't mean they couldn't—and didn't—have real illnesses. She reminded herself not to prejudge the woman based on past experiences with her.

"Mrs. Sanderson," Laura said after she sat down in the exam room, "how can I help you today?"

Whether consciously or unconsciously, the woman's hand went to her chest. "I think I'm having heart attacks."

"What makes you say that?"

"I have this terrible pain in my chest. It lasts for maybe half an hour each time."

"How often does this occur?"

"Perhaps twice a week," the patient replied.

"Does anything seem to bring it on?"

"It's usually after I eat, most often the evening meal. At first I thought it was just indigestion, but an antacid didn't do much for it."

Laura asked more questions and learned that the pain was centered in Mrs. Sanderson's chest, didn't radiate to her arm or jaw, was unassociated with sweating or weakness, and didn't seem to prevent her from being active.

"Let's do a cardiogram," Laura said. "If these episodes are truly problems with your heart, they might have produced some changes we can see on the EKG."

She called Courtney to do the tracing, as well as draw some blood for enzyme tests that would indicate any active heart damage.

While Courtney was busy with Mrs. Sanderson, Laura examined and treated two other patients. One had turned her ankle the day before, and after checking an X-ray to rule out a fracture, Laura instructed the patient in a regimen of elevation, alternating ice and heat, and use of an ankle brace and cane. "I don't think you'll need to see an orthopedist," Laura said. "Let me know if it's not better in a few days, or call immediately if it worsens."

The other patient was a teenager whose mother insisted he come in to be checked before leaving with a youth group for a brief ski trip. He hadn't been eating well, and when pressed, admitted he'd had some abdominal pain. His temperature was slightly elevated, and a white blood count indicated an active infection. Laura elicited rebound tenderness of his abdomen—some pain on pressing in, and even more pain when pressure was released. Not only that, the pain was most pronounced in the right lower quadrant of his abdomen.

"Johnny, I think you may have appendicitis," Laura said to the teen as his mother looked on.

"I can't have that," he said. "I want to go skiing with the group." He turned a desperate look toward his mother. "It's just a bug. I'm feeling better already. I want to go on this trip."

The woman just shook her head. "Listen to the doctor."

Laura looked at his mother. "I'll put in a call to a surgeon and see if we can't get Johnny seen right away. I hope I'm wrong, but if I'm right, it's better to deal with it now than have it rupture while he's in Colorado."

By this time, Courtney had finished with the EKG on Mrs. Sanderson. Laura tapped on the exam room door and entered. She held out the tracing and said to the patient, "Your cardiogram is absolutely normal, which is good. The enzyme study results won't be back for a few hours, and I expect them to be normal as well."

"Oh, thank goodness," Mrs. Sanderson said.

"I think you're having episodes of esophageal spasm from reflux of acid—what we sometimes call GERD or gastroesophageal reflux disease."

"Is there a cure for that?"

"I'll give you medication to calm it down, but we also recommend some things you can do to help." She suggested the woman not eat within two hours of bedtime. Laura warned Mrs. Sanderson to avoid the "four C's" that could contribute to GERD: carbohydrates, carbonation, caffeine, and chocolate.

"Sleeping on two pillows often helps this," Laura said as she wound up the discussion. "I want to see you in a couple of weeks. Call earlier if you have any change." She'd saved her next recommendation for last, knowing that if she led with it, the patient might not hear anything else she said—because the fifth "C" was calories. "And you should try to drop a few pounds. This problem is most common in people who are overweight."

Robert Morris felt his cell phone buzz in his pocket. He couldn't answer it while court was in session—couldn't even sneak a peek at the caller ID.

Fifteen minutes later, the judge called for the midmorning recess. As soon as the judge left the bench, Robert looked at his phone to see who had called. There were two missed calls from the Hilton Police Department.

He hurried into the hall, found a quiet spot, and hit the button on his cell phone to return the call. "Yes, this is Robert Morris. Someone there tried to call me a few minutes ago."

"Hold a moment, please."

Silence followed. The lawyer was happy he wasn't being subjected to some awful computer-generated tones that mimicked a melody, or worse yet, some of the "music on hold" he'd encountered. Just as he looked at his watch for the third or fourth time, he heard, "Sergeant Fuller. Is this Mr. Morris?"

"Yes," he said. "I'm an attorney, and we're in the middle of a trial, so I couldn't answer your call." He pulled back his cuff and checked the time. "Matter of fact, this is only a short recess, so I'll have to make this quick. Is this about my aunt Ina?"

"Yes it is," Fuller said. "I presume your sister has told you we're investigating her death. We'd like to talk with you as soon as possible."

Robert looked around. "Look, I need to get back into the courtroom. Why don't I call you back after the court adjourns for lunch?"

The detective gave him his cell phone number. "I'll look forward to hearing from you around noon," Fuller said.

There were noises at the door of the courtroom as people started to reenter it, but before he ended the call, Robert asked, "Are you certain my aunt didn't die of natural causes?"

"Until we find evidence to the contrary," Fuller said, "this is a murder investigation."

It was lunchtime, but Laura really wasn't hungry. Her mind was on Aunt Ina's death—both the sense of loss associated with the death of the last living relative of her late mother, and thoughts of the tasks that lay before her as she made her aunt's final arrangements.

She got a cold Dr Pepper from the office refrigerator and sipped it while she scanned articles from the stack of professional journals balanced on the edge of her desk. Laura was having a hard time remembering what she'd read and was about to give up when her cell phone buzzed. That would be Carter, calling around lunchtime, as he tried to do each day.

After a sentence or two of preliminary conversation, she broke the news to him that not only had Aunt Ina been found dead that morning, the police also thought she'd been murdered.

"Oh, Laura. I'm so sorry to hear about this," Carter said to his wife. Even though he was probably alone, Laura noticed that he lowered his voice. "You're sure the police think it was murder?"

"That's what the sergeant who called said. I'm going down to the police station in a few minutes to give them a statement."

"Let me see if I can postpone my next case, and I'll meet you there," Carter said.

"No need. I'm perfectly capable of giving them a statement. I'll just stick to what Mark Twain once said—'If I tell the truth, I don't need to remember what I said.'"

She could just picture Carter's smile. "You should have been a surgeon," he said. "You're absolutely unflappable under pressure. Anyway, I've got to get back into the OR. With the

New Year's holiday coming up, it seems that everyone who needs elective surgery wants theirs done today."

Before they ended the conversation, Laura heard a tinny voice in the background. "Dr. Hawkins, your next patient is coming into the room now."

"Well, I've got to go," Carter said. "Call me when you get through with the police."

"I will, but I don't think there's going to be a problem." She hung up, wondering why she'd said that. Because Laura had the distinct feeling there would be problems ahead for her and some others before all this was wrapped up.

Laura had never been in a police station. This one in Hilton, Texas, probably bore little resemblance to the larger ones she'd seen on TV programs like *Blue Bloods*, but it was large enough and unfamiliar enough to add to her nervousness at being there.

"Doctor, thank you for coming."

The man headed toward her wore a police uniform with three stripes on the sleeve, and she was pretty sure his was the voice she'd heard on the phone earlier that morning. The sergeant was older than any of the other officers she'd seen in the building—probably early sixties. He was short and heavyset, with a serious expression. Then again, she doubted that he came in contact with many things that made him smile.

"I'm Sergeant Jason Fuller," the man said, extending his hand to Laura, who shook it. "Thanks for coming. I'm sorry for your loss." He pointed to an empty office. "Can we sit down for just a minute? I need to ask you some questions."

"I guess this is silly, but are you sure the person you found dead is Aunt Ina?"

"Yes. As I told you, we had the picture on her driver's license, as well as some of the pictures and papers inside the house. There's no doubt about her identity. I'm sorry."

Laura felt the last tiny shred of hope she'd harbored flee. Oh well. Aunt Ina had lived a full life. Her husband had been dead for almost ten years. Laura recalled her aunt saying many times, "When I die, it's just a matter of moving from this temporary existence to my permanent home in Heaven."

The room to which Fuller led her contained a table with two chairs on either side. She took one of the chairs facing the door and watched as a young woman in a police uniform followed Fuller into the room. The two officers sat across from Laura. Fuller indicated the woman beside him. "Officer Adela Reyes will be joining us. She discovered the body of your aunt."

"I'm sorry for your loss," Reyes said. "Can I get you something? Water? Coffee?"

"I'm fine," Laura said. Then she looked at Fuller. "What can I tell you?"

The sergeant reached toward the tape recorder that sat on center of the table. "I'd like to record this, if I may. But first, I need to advise you of your rights." He then proceeded to recite the usual admonition about the right to remain silent, the right to an attorney, and so forth.

"Why do I get a Miranda warning?" Laura asked.

"Just routine," Fuller said with a straight face.

"Doesn't seem routine to me," Laura said. "It seems like an interrogation rather than a simple interview. Should I call a lawyer and have him present?"

"That's up to you," Fuller said. "As I said, this is just routine."

After a moment's thought, Laura decided she didn't need legal representation. After all, she hadn't done anything wrong. "For now, why don't you ask your questions? If I think I need a lawyer, I'll put a stop to the interview."

"Fair enough," Fuller said. "To begin with, we need to know when you last saw your aunt alive."

"Why is that important?" Laura asked.

"Well, there were no witnesses to her death, and the fact that her body lay in the snow for so long that it was pretty frozen makes it hard to establish time of death. When we know who last saw her alive, we can start checking the alibis of all our suspects."

"Alibis? Suspects? Who are your suspects? Am I one?"

Fuller took his time answering. Finally, he said, "Right now, everyone is a suspect. But we always look first at the family."

The implications of the policeman's words washed over Laura like an ice-cold wave. Aunt Ina Bell was dead. She probably had been murdered. And the murderer might be one of her family members. How much worse could it get?

3

The snow had stopped, the sun was out, and the Fort Worth streets were clearing nicely. Traffic was light, and Robert's car purred along smoothly. The trial had wound up shortly after lunch, with the jury deliberating for less than two hours before returning a verdict for his client. The award was massive. Of course, so were the attorney's fees, but his client would be happy to pay them after winning such a victory.

Robert looked at the clock on the dashboard of his car. He needed to talk with the managing partner of his firm, preferably in person. Surely after the work he'd done in winning this case, the executive committee would grant him a bonus. Perhaps they'd elevate him to partner status, with the bump in compensation that accompanied it.

Maybe that would finally satisfy Claudia. Their home was more than large enough for Robert, but Claudia often said it felt "cramped" when they entertained large groups. They were members of one of Fort Worth's nicest country clubs, but Claudia had heard of another one that opened recently. Of course, the new one had an initiation fee larger than the cost of Robert's first car, but she begged him to join. It seemed to him she was never satisfied.

Then again, he'd wanted a trophy wife, and Claudia certainly filled the bill. After his graduation from law school, he had taken the offer of this firm in Fort Worth, put in hours that would kill a lesser man, and eventually risen to his present status. Claudia had been there with him every step of the way. Perhaps this was the pinnacle she'd sought—for him and for her. He hoped so.

He was halfway to the office, when his cell phone rang. He glanced at the face of the phone and saw the call was from the Hilton Police Department. He'd promised to call that sergeant—he had his name written down somewhere—when court broke for lunch, but Robert had been so caught up in the trial that he'd forgotten. He answered the call, using his Bluetooth. "Robert Morris."

"Mr. Morris, this is Sergeant Fuller of the Hilton Police Department. I didn't get a call at lunch. Since you're answering, I presume court has adjourned for the day."

"Oh, yes, Sergeant. The judge had the lawyers in his chambers for most of the lunch break, arguing a point of law." *It's a safe enough lie. I doubt that he'll check up on me.* "But the case just wound up. Now, I believe you had some questions for me about my late aunt."

"Right. When can you make it over here to talk with me?"

Robert frowned. The idea of visiting a police station, especially one thirty miles away from where he lived, wasn't on his agenda for the immediate future. "Sergeant, I don't know how much the snow has melted on the roads between here and there. Isn't there some way we could do this by phone?"

"No sir. I need to sit down face-to-face and get the answers to some questions."

"Well . . ." Robert said.

The sergeant was silent. Obviously, the ball was in Robert's court. Finally, he said, "I need to clear some time on my calendar. I suppose I could drive over in a week or so. Would that work?"

"No, sir, it won't. How about midmorning tomorrow, at our offices?" The sergeant paused for a beat. "If you feel you can't get away, or if you're afraid to trust the roads, I could come to your law offices in Fort Worth tomorrow morning. Of course, if I did that, I'd probably end up having to bring a couple of uniformed policemen with me. We could march in, sit down at your desk—with the door open, of course— and spend a couple of hours questioning you. Would that be better?"

Robert knew when he was beaten. "No, no. That won't be necessary. I'll see you at the Hilton PD headquarters about ten tomorrow."

"I'll look forward to it," the sergeant said, a smile in his voice.

Robert grimaced as he steered into his reserved parking space at the office building his firm occupied. If he hurried, maybe the office New Year's party would still be going on. But when he entered the firm's suite, the receptionist told him the party had ended an hour ago, and he'd just missed the managing partner.

"Well, I guess I'll go home," Robert said. "I'll just call him. I know he'll want to hear the details of this case."

Fuller leaned back in his desk chair and grinned.

"I ought to be looking for feathers floating around," Reyes said. "You look like the cat that swallowed the canary."

The sergeant turned to where she sat at a vacant desk nearby. "I just got to put a lawyer on the spot. I probably should take it easy on the guy, but I have the impression Robert Morris wasn't too broken up over the death of his aunt." He grinned. "And I know why."

"Why is that?" Reyes asked.

"While you were finishing the paperwork that goes with the discovery of Ina Bell Patrick's body, I've been getting a report on the dead woman's finances."

"How'd you go about that?"

"I made a few phone calls. There are five banks in town, and I found Ms. Patrick's account at the third one I called. Want to guess how much money she left?"

"I don't know," Reyes said. "Maybe a couple of thousand dollars?"

"Put some zeroes after that," Fuller said. "She carried about a thousand in her checking account, another four or so in a money market savings account."

"You make it sound like there's more. Is there?"

"You might say so. She had laddered certificates of deposit with the bank, to the tune of two million dollars total." Fuller grinned. "Think about it. Her late husband was a successful insurance agent, so there's no doubt in my mind she got a substantial amount of money from the policies he carried. She's lived in that house since they got married, so it's probably been paid off for a while. From what I can tell after talking to a few people, Ms. Patrick lived simply and spent very little. She got monthly payments from Social Security and maybe an annuity or two. She might have tapped some of the proceeds of the insurance settlement, but she saved most of her money."

"Now who gets it?" Reyes asked. "Her niece and nephew?"

"Probably. And that begs the question you should always ask when investigating a murder. *Cui bono?* Who benefits?"

No one likes to be on hold, and Dr. Bruce Goldman was no exception. The pathologist sat in his office and drummed his fingers on the top of his desk. He stole a glance at the calendar and smiled. Tomorrow was New Year's Eve, and he was going to leave early. Even though, to alter the phrase from literature a bit, death didn't take a holiday at that time—matter of fact, there'd be plenty of corpses from car wrecks and a few ODs for his staff to autopsy—because he was the chief, he made out the schedule. And he intended to leave at noon tomorrow, spend the long weekend in front of the TV set watching football, and forget about this place for a while.

Goldman caught a cold breeze and a whiff of formalin, and despite thirty years in the profession, he wrinkled his nose. A door slammed, and he realized that someone had just come out of the morgue, which was right down the hall from his office. He sighed. *I'm getting too old for this. It's time to retire.*

The pathologist was brought back from his daydreams by an electronic voice. "This is Sergeant Fuller. Sorry you had to hold."

Goldman switched the phone to his other hand and identified himself.

"Bruce, it seems as though the only time we talk, it's about corpses and autopsy results. Please tell me this is a social call."

"Afraid not," Goldman said. "But maybe after the first of the year, you and Lily can come over to our place for dinner."

"That would be nice," Fuller said. "But I'm betting you didn't call just to talk about getting together for dinner some evening. What's up?"

"It's about that half-frozen corpse you sent over." Goldman shuffled through some papers on his desk. "Ina Bell Patrick."

"Don't tell me you've done the autopsy already," Fuller said. "You couldn't have gotten the body more than a few hours ago."

"No, we're going to have to wait until tomorrow for complete thawing. But I did a preliminary external examination, which is the reason for my call. I saw definite evidence of a blow to the head—right occipital region."

"Where's that in English?"

"Back of the head, on the right," Goldman said. "If I had to guess, I'd say that when I get in there I'll find an epidural hematoma. Pressure from the accumulation of blood shut down the vital centers, killing her. It's conceivable this was an accident, but that will depend on circumstances. I'll leave that up to you to determine."

"What if I told you we found her in her front yard, lying buried faceup in a mound of snow as if someone had laid her out."

"Well, she didn't hit her head on the snow and die, that's for sure. So you're thinking homicide? That would certainly work."

"What about time of death?"

"You're going to have to tell us when she was last seen alive," the pathologist said. "It would have been convenient if she was wearing a watch that hit something and broke, but that didn't happen."

"Can you tell anything from rigor mortis and things like that?" Fuller asked.

"Since her body was essentially frozen, none of that helps. Of course, at autopsy we can have a look at the stomach contents, but until we know when she had her last meal, we can't make any assumptions. So the ball's in your court."

"We're still questioning people to determine who last saw her alive," Fuller said. "Will you let me know when the autopsy's completed?"

"I plan on doing that exam first thing in the morning," Goldman said. "I hope to be out of this place by noon tomorrow, but I'll call you before I leave."

After he hung up, Goldman made a few notes on one of the forms on his desk. Then he started to think about the long holiday weekend coming up. While he was watching bowl games on TV, Fuller and his colleagues would be working to find the person who killed Ina Bell Patrick. *I guess my life could be worse.*

Fay Autrey sat on the edge of the chair in front of Sergeant Fuller's desk. "I've never been in a police station before," she said.

"Nothing to be worried about," the sergeant said. He adjusted his reading glasses. "I just want to go over this statement you gave Officer Reyes."

"Anything I can do to help," Ms. Autrey said.

"According to this, you and Ms. Patrick had a light supper together last night. That would be on Tuesday, December twenty-ninth. Is that correct?"

"Yes."

"So she was alive at that time. Officer Reyes found her body after three this morning, so that was maybe nine hours after you last saw her. Right?"

"That would be about right. I left her about six, and didn't know anything about her death . . ." She dabbed at her eyes with a handkerchief. "I had no idea what happened to poor Ina until Officer Reyes knocked on my door about midmorning."

"Do you have a key to Ms. Patrick's house?"

"Uh, no." Autrey paused. "Why do you ask?"

"It's just unusual, if you were best friends. I mean, quite often neighbors exchange house keys. And what if you ran an errand for her, and the door was locked when you came back?"

"I guess Ina was just too private a person to let anyone have a key—even me," Autrey said.

Fuller went over the woman's story one more time, but it stayed consistent. "That's it, I guess," he said. "Thank you for coming."

After she left, Reyes, who had been sitting nearby, said, "Why did you ask her about a key?"

"You and I didn't do a thorough search of Ms. Patrick's house after you found the body. We looked inside long enough to find some identification. Then I took the key ring I found, locked the house, and left. But at the station, I gave the key to a couple of officers and asked them to do a more thorough search. It looked to them as if the front door had been forced, and someone had been searching the place."

"Was something missing?"

"No way to tell. But whoever did it was in a hurry. Judging by a few outlines in dust on some surfaces, the searcher didn't put things back exactly where they'd been. And whatever he or she was looking for was fairly small. If the person who did the searching had a key, they wouldn't have forced the lock like that."

Reyes nodded. "Interesting."

Fuller pulled a pad toward him and added what he'd found out to the timeline he'd started. Ina Bell Patrick's niece had last talked with her by phone on the day after Christmas. Her nephew, Robert, had called her and spoken briefly a couple of days before Christmas, but not since. The last time

Ms. Patrick had been seen alive was by Fay Autrey in the early evening of December 29.

"Reyes," he called.

The officer looked up from the crime scene photos she had spread out on the desk. "Yes?"

"Our victim's time of death looks like it will be sometime between six p.m. the night of December twenty-ninth and the time you found her on December thirtieth. Why don't you get started double-checking alibis for that time?"

Robert Morris leaned back in his favorite recliner and closed his eyes. Claudia had taken one look at him when he came home and hurried off to cancel the dinner plans she'd made. But he knew there'd be others.

Claudia was a social animal, and she wasn't about to stop until she reached the pinnacle of Fort Worth society. Unfortunately, this meant that she and Robert spent most evenings at the opera or theatre, sometimes having dinner with other "power" couples, either at the country club or at one of their homes.

Robert opened his eyes when he heard Claudia enter the room. She held their cordless phone. "Robert, your sister is calling." She handed him the phone and disappeared out the door.

"Hello, Laura," he said without much enthusiasm.

"Robert, have you talked with Sergeant Fuller?"

"I spoke with him very briefly during the morning recess. Then he called back this afternoon and sort of bullied me into taking time tomorrow to drive to Hilton to sit down with him. I'm not certain why it's so important that he speak with me right now."

"As I recall from what little forensic pathology I had in med school, if a person's been frozen, it makes it difficult to tell when they died. The police probably want to check your alibi for Thursday night, when she was found, as well as any information you can give about when you last saw her."

Was Laura getting in a dig? Sure, he'd said he and Claudia would be at Aunt Ina's for Christmas dinner, but they'd changed their minds. Laura, the good niece, had been there with Carter, of course. Good for them. And what about Zack? That lost sheep had been out of touch for nearly five years, and, as far as Robert was concerned, he could stay gone.

"Well, I'm going to drive over, give whatever statement they want, and come back to Fort Worth."

"Want to get together for lunch while you're in Hilton tomorrow?" Laura asked.

"No, I'm going to have to make this a quick trip. But I'm sure Claudia would like you and Carter to come over some evening." *And if my sister takes me up on this, there's another little tiff I'm going to have with Claudia.*

"I'll call her in a few days," Laura said. "Maybe after the dust settles from Aunt Ina's . . . I started to say 'death,' but I guess I should call it by its right name. Her murder."

"We'll see," Robert said.

"Are you going to need a lawyer with you tomorrow?" she asked.

"Laura, I *am* a lawyer," he said.

"Robert, you haven't done any criminal work since you got your law degree. And I doubt you've ever been inside a police station."

"Nevertheless, I know enough not to put my foot in anything." He looked up and saw Claudia in the doorway. "I believe dinner is ready. I'll call you soon."

Despite Carter's offer to take her out, Laura said she'd rather cook something at home. She was in the kitchen, stirring a pot of spaghetti sauce, when the phone rang. "Carter, would you get that?"

The phone stopped ringing, and Laura heard the low buzz of Carter talking. After probably five minutes, he hung up, and she heard him head back down the hall. She started to call to him and ask about the phone call, but decided that the food would be ready soon. She'd ask him when they sat down to eat.

In a moment, he appeared in the kitchen door. "Smells good. Want me to set the table?"

"Please," Laura said. "And you could put together a salad if you want to."

She watched out of the corner of her eye as Carter shredded lettuce and added cubes of tomato to the bowl. When he almost took out a thumb shredding carrots over the salad, she asked, "How come you're such a good surgeon and such a lousy cook?" She made sure to smile to take the sting out of her remark.

"Sorry, I guess I'm preoccupied."

"Who was that on the phone? You talked too long for it to be a phone solicitor. Was it a patient?"

Carter dropped the shredder in the sink and set tongs in the salad he'd prepared. "No. It was Mitzi."

"What did she want?"

"It's hard to say. I guess she wanted to talk with you, but when I told her you were cooking, she said she'd call another time."

Mitzi was something of a family friend. The divorcée was younger than Carter and Laura, had no children living with her, and her job at the travel agency didn't seem to occupy much of her time. Laura pictured the woman—brunette hair perfectly styled, makeup just right, clothes showing off a figure most women (including Laura) envied.

Mitzi usually called about once a week, but since Aunt Ina's death she'd phoned more often. Laura made a mental note to call her friend back sometime soon. But right now, she was more interested in having a quiet meal with her husband. She wasn't sure how many more they'd have until the police solved the mystery of how Aunt Ina died.

4

It was noon on Thursday, December 31, and Dr. Laura Morris, miracle of miracles, was on her way out the door of the clinic where she worked. Another doctor—actually a couple of other doctors—would be on call over the next three and a half days. Of course, this didn't mean Laura had nothing to do. It simply freed her from clinical responsibilities so she could attend to everything else on her plate.

She didn't mind helping out by making final arrangements for Aunt Ina. Laura had fond memories of her aunt. Besides, who would do it if she didn't? She couldn't see Robert stepping up and helping with the funeral arrangements. As a lawyer, he could probably help get her aunt's affairs wound up. He could, but Laura figured she'd have to take the lead in that as well. She was no legal expert, but Laura felt certain that, in the absence of a will, her aunt's estate would pass to her niece and nephews. Actually, both nephews, she guessed, although it had been almost five years since Zack was around.

What about selling Aunt Ina's house? Should she shut off the utilities? Was there food in the refrigerator that might spoil? And could Laura legally take care of any of this? She wished her aunt had left a will. Maybe the police would find one soon.

Laura had almost reached her car when her cell phone rang. Oh, please, not the clinic. The caller ID didn't help— "anonymous caller." Despite her better judgment, Laura answered.

"Doctor Morris, forgive me for calling on your cell phone, but the clinic said you'd already left. I got this number from Ina's address book."

"Who is this?" Laura asked.

"Oh, I'm sorry. This is Fay Autrey—your aunt's best friend."

Laura had heard her aunt mention Fay Autrey, but she wasn't sure about the "best friend" designation. Laura knew the woman lived two houses down from Aunt Ina, and when Ina finally decided she shouldn't try to drive anymore, her "friend" dropped off dry cleaning and picked up groceries for her. According to what she'd heard from her aunt that seemed to be the extent of the "friendship."

"Hang on a second. I'm almost at my car. Give me a moment," Laura said.

Laura climbed in and started the engine in order to let the heater work. A lot of the snow had melted, but the outside temperature was still hovering in the lower forties. She fastened her seat belt and the *ding-ding* of the warning bell stopped.

"That's better," Laura said. "You were Aunt Ina's neighbor. I understand you ran errands for her sometimes."

"Oh, yes," Ms. Autrey replied. "Your aunt was an independent type, and she hated to ask me to do these things, but I was happy to."

"How often did that happen?"

"Oh, maybe every week or two. Your Aunt Ina had one of those big chest-type freezers in her garage, and she kept it filled with food. I'd bring her produce, milk, and other perishables every week or so, as well as replenish the frozen food. And the few times she needed something dropped off or picked up from the cleaners, I was happy to help out."

"Did she ever go to church? I remember her mentioning the Methodist Church here in town."

"Yes, perhaps once a month she'd ride with me to church. But I know she sent them a check every month, whether she went or not."

And here it comes. She's managed to introduce money into the conversation. Laura decided to let it go right past her. "Well, it was good of you to call, Ms. Autrey, but I have a lot of things to do now. I'll be sure you'll be notified about Aunt Ina's service."

"Thank you, dear. I wanted to ask, though, if you or any of those police I've seen around your aunt's house have found her will yet."

"They haven't found one," Laura said. "Or, if they have, I haven't heard about it."

"Oh, that can't be right," Autrey said. "She told me on a number of occasions that she was going to leave me a large sum of money in her will. Her exact words were 'I couldn't forget my best friend. You'll be surprised when you see my will. I'm going to see that you're well taken care of.' There's got to be a will. They just haven't found it yet."

"Mary, this is Dr. Morris. Is my husband available?"

"He's still in the OR. An emergency case came in, and he added it after the one he had scheduled," the nurse said. "He'll be calling us before he leaves the hospital to come to the office. Do you want to leave a message?"

"No, don't bother him. He'll probably call me right after he calls you. Thanks."

Laura wanted to talk with Carter about Fay Autrey, but it could wait. In the meantime, she'd fix herself a light lunch— maybe some soup and a half-sandwich.

She was just chewing the last bite of sandwich, when the phone rang—not her cell, which was the one Carter usually called, but the landline. She wasn't on call, but it might be the clinic. Laura sighed, used her napkin, and then hurried to the living room, where the phone continued to ring.

"Hello?"

"Laura? This is Mitzi. Is Carter at home too? I thought perhaps I might catch you both."

"No, Carter's still doing a case." Laura knew she should talk with her friend, but she just didn't want to take the time today. Mitzi, on the other hand, had lots of time, and was likely to call anytime the spirit moved her. Sometimes these conversations had been nice—a relaxing break from the responsibilities of the day. But today Laura had too much on her mind. This wasn't a good time to talk.

"I appreciate your calling, but I have a lot going on right now," Laura said. "You understand, don't you?"

"Of course," Mitzi said. "Do you and Carter have any plans for New Year's Day? I'm having a few friends over tomorrow to watch some of the Bowl games, and wondered if maybe you'd like to come over here."

"I don't know, Mitzi. Look, I appreciate your concern, but I have a lot to do."

"Well, I won't keep you. Just know that I'm here," Mitzi said.

After she hung up, Laura replayed the conversation in her head. Had the purpose of Mitzi's call been to talk with her, or did she simply cover up her intent when Laura answered instead of Carter? *Don't be ridiculous. You're jumping to conclusions.* Nevertheless, she filed the information away, vowing to keep a closer eye on her friend . . . and her husband.

Robert Morris stood with two coats over his arm, waiting for his wife to finish her round of good-byes. The New Year's Eve party at their country club would undoubtedly continue for several more hours, finally moving on to a breakfast of scrambled eggs and mimosas at the home of one of the members, after which the "beautiful people" would go home to sleep off their New Year's excesses.

Despite her protests that it was still early, Robert had told Claudia it was time for them to go home. Correction: it was time for *him* to leave, and she was coming with him. It was already after one in the morning. How could these people party that long?

At last, Claudia joined him. He helped her on with the fur coat he'd bought her two years ago, then slipped on his own cashmere topcoat. When they were in their car on the way home, she said, "That was a wonderful party. Aren't you glad we joined this club? Isn't it so much better than our old one?"

Robert shook his head. Claudia really wasn't asking for his opinion. She was simply gearing up for conversations she'd have with a number of her friends over the days and weeks to come. They probably wouldn't really be conversations—more like monologues. In them, she'd list the important people at the party, describe how nice the country club was, and in general brag about how her husband was advancing in his profession so he could afford nice things like tonight.

His thoughts went briefly to the bonus he'd hoped to get for winning the case he'd just concluded. He'd called the managing partner of his firm on his way home yesterday. "I'm sorry to miss the New Year's celebration at the firm. And, honestly, I wanted to hear your reaction about my winning that big verdict."

"Oh, yes, that was nice work," Mr. Smithers had said. "I was going to tell you this when I saw you in person, but since you brought it up—the partners have decided we can't afford to give bonuses right now, even to you, despite the case you just won."

"What about promotion to partner?" Robert asked.

"We can discuss that later."

Robert knew what Smithers meant by that. He meant "No."

Had Claudia already spent that bonus? If she hadn't, she probably had plans to do so. How was he going to keep enough money coming in? If Aunt Ina's estate was big enough, he could leave and set up his own firm. But what if he didn't get the amount he anticipated?

Robert was keeping his head above water by putting in sixty-hour weeks at the office, and he knew he wasn't the only person in the world doing just that—making good money but still living from paycheck to paycheck. He felt like one of the performers he recalled seeing years ago at the circus—performers who set a number of plates spinning on upright wooden rods. Just as he got one plate going, another would begin to wobble until the performer sprinted to it and gave it another spin. That had become Robert's life. Sometimes he wondered what might happen if one of the plates fell. He hoped he didn't find out the hard way.

It was nearing noon on New Year's Day. Laura figured some of the population of Hilton would still be sleeping, a few of them nursing hangovers. She and Carter had decided a few years ago to start spending New Year's Eve at home, and that's what they had done last night. They awoke later than usual this morning and had a leisurely breakfast.

They were still at the kitchen table when Carter stood and looked at his watch. "I'm going to make rounds. It shouldn't take long," he said.

Laura kissed him good-bye, then settled down with a third cup of coffee and the morning paper. When the doorbell rang, she said to herself, "That will be Robert." She put down her section of the newspaper and headed for the front door.

She opened the door and admitted her brother. "I'm glad you could come over," she said, trying to make the emotion behind it genuine.

Robert didn't answer. He simply walked in, shucked his overcoat and gloves—tossing them on the living room sofa—and sat down beside her. His expression said it all: I didn't want to go out in freezing weather on New Year's Day, I didn't want to make a thirty-minute drive over here, and I certainly didn't want to put up with Claudia's harangue when I told her where I was going.

Laura could read Robert's expression, if not his thoughts. "I know you didn't want to do this," she said, "but we really need to talk, and I thought this was something better dealt with face-to-face."

"Well, let's have it," Robert said.

"Sergeant Fuller called late yesterday. The police have searched Aunt Ina's house. They checked with the lawyers they were able to contact here in town. So far as they can tell, she died intestate."

"So?" Robert said.

"Robert, you're a lawyer. Did you ever talk with Aunt Ina about drawing up a will?"

"I offered to help her get one done. I gave her some advice on making bequests. But so far as I know, she never acted on any of it."

"Here's where I need your legal opinion," Laura said. "Someone has to arrange for a funeral home to pick up Aunt Ina's body from the medical examiner's office, plan a memorial service, and probably do half a dozen more things. Who has the authority to do that?"

"In the absence of anyone else coming forward, I imagine your proceeding would be permitted."

"And her estate?" Laura asked. "How is that handled?"

Robert's manner went from sullen to pedantic as he leaned forward and used his fingers to enumerate his points. "First, a thorough search must be made for a will. Second, if one isn't found, the decedent is presumed to have died intestate. In which case, there are a number of scenarios for division of the property."

"I don't need a lesson as though you were preparing me for the bar exam. Just tell me what happens in this particular case. Neither Aunt Ina's parents or grandparents are alive. Her husband was an only child, and he's dead. There are no children from their marriage. It seems to me that the estate would be divided among Aunt Ina's niece and nephews: me, you, and Zack."

"That's the court's decision, but you're most likely right." He leaned back on the sofa. "Although, some effort would have to be made to find Zack, my guess is that the long-lost black sheep of the family will never turn up. In which case, the third of Aunt Ina's estate held in escrow for him would be divided between you and me."

Was that a smile creeping across her brother's face? Laura knew her sibling's wife was spending money as fast as he could earn it. Maybe he saw this as an opportunity to get a little ahead. Whether he let Claudia know the full extent of the inheritance . . . well, that was up to Robert.

"So what do we do now?" Laura asked. "We—" She was interrupted by the doorbell. "I wonder who that could be. I'm not expecting anyone." She rose. "Excuse me."

At the door, she looked through the side window. The man standing on her porch appeared vaguely familiar—not so much his body habitus as his face. Her eyes were drawn to the scar that went across the left side of his face, from his cheek to the corner of his mouth. When she put aside the scar, though, the face tickled at her memory.

He was tall and thin, his long blond hair unruly, with a scraggly beard adding to his already disheveled appearance. Snow dotted his bare head. His hands were thrust into the pockets of a wrinkled fatigue jacket that had seen better days. His jeans were faded and ragged, with both knees showing through. He looked to be maybe five or six years younger than Laura—probably in his late-twenties.

She opened the door. "Yes?"

"Sis, how about a hug for your long-lost brother?"

5

Laura couldn't believe it. The stranger on her doorstep was Zack, her younger brother. Here was the man she'd thought she might never see again. True, it wasn't the Zack she remembered, but a lot of things could explain the changes in his appearance. What counted was her brother was back home.

Laura embraced him, responding to his words, while her brain tried to process this new information. Her brother's build had been athletic, while this man was thin—almost painfully so. Zack had been clean-shaven and had kept his blond hair short, but that was hardly a description that fit the man on the doorstep. And the scar—Zack certainly had no such scar on his face. There had to be a story behind all that.

"I'm sorry, Zack," she said. "Is it really you? I just wasn't expecting . . . I mean, it's been so . . ." Laura gave free rein to the tears forming in her eyes. "I've got a million questions. But come in out of the cold. Robert's here."

When Zack entered the living room, Robert looked at him with vague interest, but there was no spark of recognition in his eyes.

"This is our brother, Zack," Laura said. "He's back."

At first, there was no reaction from Robert. He seemed to process the information, and after he did, it seemed to Laura that the temperature in the room dropped noticeably—and not just because the front door had been open for a bit.

Robert didn't stand up and embrace his younger brother. Instead, he nodded once and said, "Zack—if you are Zack— it's so nice of you to come back. I can see that you've prospered while you were gone."

Zack didn't rise to the bait. "I guess I look a lot different than what you remember. And I suppose I should. I've got quite a story to tell," he replied.

"I'm sure you do," Robert said. "You're just in time to get your share of Aunt Ina's estate. Then I suppose you'll be leaving town again."

Zack took a seat on the couch next to Robert and said, "I heard about Aunt Ina's death, so I got here as quickly as I could." He looked down at his clothing. "I must look terrible. I've been traveling for a couple of days. I can't count how many busses I've been on."

Laura settled into a chair at a right angle to the sofa where her two brothers sat. "How did you find out about Aunt Ina's death?" she asked.

"Fay—that is, Ms. Autrey—told me."

"She didn't mention that to me when I talked with her yesterday."

"I asked her to keep it a secret," Zack said. "I wanted to surprise you."

Robert's eyes narrowed. "We haven't seen you in almost five years. I'll admit that there's a vague resemblance to my younger brother, although you're thinner than I remember, and the hair's different. And your face . . . Do you have something that proves your identity?"

Zack reached into the hip pocket of his worn jeans and removed a wallet. He opened it to show a Nevada driver's license. "I'll admit, the picture isn't very good, but then again, those never are."

"That tells me you have Zack's wallet, but it doesn't tell me you're really him," Robert said. "How do we know you're really Zack?"

Zack nodded as though he understood. "Fingerprints won't do it, because I've never been printed." He frowned. "I'd offer to play twenty questions, but I have to admit I did some drugs before I got my life turned around, so my memory isn't what it used to be." He pointed to the scar on his face. "And, yes, I've been in a few bar fights too. Fractured cheekbone, broken nose, this cut across the face. I don't guess I look the way you remember me."

"Drugs—a very convenient excuse for any lapses of memory," Robert said.

Zack removed his fatigue jacket, revealing a dirty, wrinkled denim shirt underneath. His motions were deliberate as he rolled up the left sleeve. At the crook of his elbow, he silently pointed to several scars. "Needle tracks," he said. "I'm not proud of them, but there they are."

"Pretty nonspecific," Robert said. "But since you've rolled up your sleeves, let's try this. When he was younger, Zack got a tattoo—actually, two of them. He had barbed wire encircling his upper arms. I didn't like them then, but they might come in handy now. Why don't you show us those tattoos?"

Zack was quiet for a moment. Then, slowly, he rolled his left sleeve up further, exposing a barbed-wire tattoo around his arm. He repeated the process on the right, with the same results.

Robert's face bore an expression like he was sucking a lemon. "Maybe you really are my brother. Where were you all this time?"

Zack rolled down his sleeves and slipped back into his jacket. "I went to Las Vegas, and I partied. I didn't think about how much I was spending. Why worry? I had plenty of money. At first a luxury hotel gave me a suite for free because I was a big player in their casino. I got free drinks, a free buffet. They treated me like a big shot. Life was good."

"But then . . ." Laura said.

"But eventually the money ran out. And when I didn't have the money to spend, the management strongly suggested I leave. Actually, they sent a couple of guys to my room to encourage me do it."

"You mean they threw you out," Laura said.

"Well, yeah. So, I moved into a cheaper hotel, but it wasn't long before they wanted their money. I moved on, each place a little worse than the one before. And at every place I eventually skipped out on my rent. Finally, I started living on the street, barely getting by with handouts and doing whatever I needed to bring in a few bucks." Zack lowered his head. "By then, I was doing drugs—when I could get my hands on them."

"So you've been like the prodigal son, spending your money on riotous living," Robert said.

"I suppose," Zack said calmly. "But one day I heard about a place in town where people like me could go for help. It was a center run by a church. I had a hard time believing it—I was unkempt, begging where I could, sometimes stealing when I had to, generally looking for my next fix. But I found out it was true—the people at that church cared for me."

Zack paused, but no one said anything. "They got me into rehab, and I came out clean. Then one of the people on the staff helped me find a place to stay. They had a counselor at the center, and he helped me get a job. I found a roommate to share expenses. I didn't make much, but I was able to put aside a little money. More than that, I started to get back my self-respect."

"And you didn't contact us?" Laura asked.

"I figured that Robert wrote me off when I left. You seemed to care, but you had your own life with Carter, so I didn't want to bother you. But I talked with Aunt Ina before I left, and she made me promise to stay in touch with her. I did—for a while."

"Zack—" Laura said.

He shook his head. "When I started getting myself turned around, I wrote Aunt Ina to tell her about it. And she wrote me back—said she was proud of me. She told me to call her collect every week or so, and I did."

"How did you learn Aunt Ina had been killed?" Laura asked.

"I got busy with a temp job around Christmas, so I didn't make my usual call to her. Then Ms. Autrey called and told me what had happened. I borrowed enough money for my fare and set out for Hilton. I think I changed busses three times, but here I am." He looked directly at his brother. "I guess you're right, Robert. I am the prodigal son. And now I've returned."

When Carter Hawkins opened the door to find his wife and her brother in serious conversation with a man he didn't know, the first thought in his mind was, "Why did Laura let someone like that in the house?" Yet here she was, talking comfortably with him. Robert, on the other hand, was sending obvious signals that said, "I wish this weren't happening."

Laura looked up at her husband and said, "Carter, he's changed a lot, but this is Zack. He heard Aunt Ina had died, and he came back." Her words were delivered in an appropriately happy tone, but Carter was familiar with the expression accompanying them. His wife was still trying to figure out exactly what was going on. Well, for that matter, so was he.

Carter nodded and reached for the hand that Zack extended. He shook it, then fought the urge to hurry to the downstairs lavatory and wash up.

"I know this is a surprise," Zack said. "Sit down, and I'll explain."

"I've heard this already," Robert said. He rose, found his coat, and said, "Laura, I'll be in touch. As far as I'm concerned, you have all the authority you need to make final arrangements for Aunt Ina. And Zack . . ." It looked as though it was almost painful for him, but he forced out the words. "Welcome home."

As soon as the door closed behind Robert, Zack said, "Sis, I'm exhausted after that long bus trip. Would it be okay—"

"Of course you can stay here," Laura said. "Use the guest room—you know where it is." She apparently realized that he'd showed up empty-handed, so she added, "I think there's a new toothbrush and razor in that bathroom. If you need anything, just let me know."

"Thanks," Zack said. He turned toward the stairs.

Carter saw that Laura was looking at him, so he guessed it was his turn. "I don't think any of my clothes will fit you, but I imagine there are a couple of stores that will be open later today—Probably Target and Walmart." He pulled out his money clip and peeled off some bills. Carter added his car keys to the cash and held it all out to Zack. "After you've had time to freshen up, why don't you see if you can find some new clothes? I think that should be enough money to get what you need."

Zack looked embarrassed. "I don't know when I'll be able to pay you back. But thanks."

Carter knew the answer to that. *I know when you'll have some money. When Aunt Ina's estate is settled.* But he didn't say it. Instead, he shrugged it off. "We're glad to have you back." He almost choked on the words, but was rewarded by the look on the face of his brother-in-law—and a few minutes later, by the smile from his wife.

Jason Fuller soon tired of the New Year's Day parades his wife enjoyed watching, and none of the college bowl games on the schedule held his interest. So, shortly after a lunch that included the black-eyed peas customarily consumed on this holiday in the South, Fuller said, "Lily, I think I'm going to the office for a while."

The office was quiet, which was fine with Fuller. He'd already told Reyes to take the day off, and he didn't call her to join him now. He enjoyed working with Reyes—her enthusiasm energized him and kept him on his toes—but today he wanted some quiet time to think. Sometimes there seemed to be no substitute for putting down the known facts of a case and shuffling them around to see if a pattern developed.

Someone had murdered Ina Bell Patrick. So he asked the usual questions—who had means, motive, and opportunity?

The means was any blunt instrument. That didn't narrow the field.

The motive was money, and in the absence of a will, that was going to go to Dr. Laura Morris and her brother, Robert Morris. The phrase "absence of a will," made him think again about the break-in and search of Ina Patrick's house. Were they looking for a will? Did they find one, but take it away when the terms didn't benefit them?

Finally came opportunity, and that was where it got sticky. Reyes and Fuller had found that everyone seemed to have a reasonable alibi for the hours leading up to when Ms. Patrick was found.

Fuller crumpled his notes and tossed them in the wastebasket. He'd start fresh tomorrow.

He was on his way out of the office, wondering if Lily was planning on sandwiches from lunch's leftover ham for their supper, when the phone on his desk rang. Fuller started to ignore it—if it was something urgent, they'd try his cell—but something, either reflex or conscience, made him turn back and answer.

"Sergeant, I'm glad I caught you. This is Dr. Laura Morris. I thought you ought to know. My brother Zack—the one who's been gone for years—showed up on our doorstep this afternoon. I thought—"

"Never mind. If he's still there, don't let him leave. I'm on my way."

Fuller thought about calling Reyes, but decided to let it slide. He could interview Zack solo. He wasn't sure what he was going to ask, but there was one thing for sure. This might be one of the missing pieces to the puzzle of Ina Bell Patrick's death.

It was growing dark when Sergeant Fuller finally left her home, and Laura felt a sense of relief as she heard his car drive away. She needed time to process everything that was happening.

Zack came into the kitchen while Laura was putting the coffee cups into the dishwasher. "Sis, I'm going to take Carter up on that offer of using his car. I imagine either Target or Walmart should have some clothes that will fit me." He gave her a brotherly hug. "And thanks for letting me stay here for a bit. I'll try not to be a bad guest."

"You're not a guest," Laura said. "You're family."

Not too long after Zack left, Laura heard the phone ring. She waited for a second ring, and when there was none, she decided it was either a wrong number or Carter had answered it. About three minutes later, he stuck his head through the kitchen door "That was the hospital. Dr. Geist is supposed to be on call today, but he's doing an emergency case, and they want me to see a patient. This shouldn't take long."

"But Zack has your car," Laura said. She inclined her head toward the hallway. "The keys to my car are in my purse." Carter's head disappeared from the doorway. She called after him, "Wear your heavy coat and gloves. It's starting to snow again."

He came back through in a moment, and opened the door from the kitchen into the garage. Laura was pleased to see that Carter was wearing a topcoat and gloves, and he'd even covered his thinning brown hair with a cloth cap. He blew her a kiss, and in a moment she heard the garage door go up and her car pull out.

Laura paused at the foot of the stairs. She probably should go up and check the linens in the guest room and adjoining bathroom, but right now she felt as though she'd gone three rounds with a contender. Instead, she went into the living room and slumped into a comfortable chair, put her feet up on the hassock in front of it, and leaned back with her eyes closed.

In a moment, she could hear the occasional *ting* that told her sleet pellets were hitting the picture window just steps away from her. The drapes were still open, and she wondered if it wouldn't be wise to close them for insulation against the cold. On the other hand, she enjoyed watching the snow as it drifted lazily to the ground. This part of Texas didn't get snow often, and it had been nice to have a white Christmas for a change.

Finally, she eased out of the chair and walked to the window. The front yard was already dusted with fresh snow, and judging from the rate at which the white flakes were falling, sometimes mixed with sleet, tomorrow morning would find the neighborhood once more a winter wonderland. She hoped Zack and Carter would get back before the roads became icy.

As she stood in front of the picture window that was the centerpiece of her living room, she reflected that it was too bad things weren't really as peaceful as they seemed while she was looking out on the snow.

Then, just as she turned away, she heard a crack from the front yard, and the window shattered, showering her with shards of glass and sending her diving for cover.

6

Laura ended up on her hands and knees in the living room, ten or twelve feet from the picture window. While she was scrambling to get further away, she heard the noise again—a flat crack, as though someone had hit two wooden boards together. Almost simultaneous with that sound, there was a thud against the far wall of the living room.

Her immediate response was to seek safety. She scuttled into the hall and out of direct line with the broken window. Laura felt a constriction in her throat. Her pulse hammered. Someone was shooting at her.

She flashed back to the episode in the hospital parking lot when the dark sedan almost ran her over. Her inclination at that time had been to ignore the obvious implication that someone wanted her dead. Laura had attributed the episode to a driver who'd had too much to drink. But there was no mistaking this. She couldn't write this off as the result of alcohol, or the weather, or careless driving. No, someone was shooting at her. They wanted to kill her.

Gradually, her pulse slowed. She shivered, not just from the cold air pouring through the window but also from fright. The shooting seemed to have stopped, but was it safe yet?

Laura didn't want to go near the window again, but with the drapes wide open and the lights on in the living room, she figured she was an ideal target if the shooter decided to continue. Heedless of the glass on the floor, she crawled toward the window until she could reach up and pull the cord, closing the drapes. Then, still crouching, she turned off the living room lights.

Now what? She scuttled to the front door and double-checked that it was locked. *Should have thought of that earlier.* Should she turn on the porch light? After a moment's hesitation, she did just that. The sidelight distorted the image she received of the front yard, but what she could see appeared normal. Time to call the police.

Laura pulled her cell phone from the pocket of her slacks and dialed 9-1-1. When the operator answered, she said, in as calm a voice as she could muster, "Someone fired two shots through my living room window. I think they were trying to kill me. I need police here—now!" Realizing she was on a cell phone, she added the address.

"Is the shooting still going on?"

"There were two shots—none since," Laura said. "I don't know if the shooter is still out there. Can you send someone? Please hurry."

"Are you injured?"

"I . . . I don't know. I don't think so." Laura felt something dribbling down her neck. She gingerly touched her head and face, and found several spicules of glass sticking out of the skin there. When she withdrew her hand, there was a streak of blood on it. She found she'd also picked up a few cuts and scrapes on her palms and knees during her crawl to safety. "I guess I've been cut by flying glass, but I can handle that—I'm a physician. Just get the police here ASAP."

Keys clicked in the background. The operator's voice was calm as she assured Laura a unit was on its way to investigate. "Are you sure you're okay?"

"No, I'm not okay. I'm scared to death," Laura almost screamed. *But I'm alive.* As for "okay," she wondered if she'd ever be okay again.

"Hang on. There should be an officer there any minute."

Laura backed further down the hall. *I ought to get something to protect myself.* She opened the door to the closet and rummaged until she found Carter's golf clubs. She took out the longest one, a club with a large metal head. Should she choose a shorter one? No, more length meant more power if she had to swing it, and more distance between her and her attacker.

"What's keeping the police?" she asked the operator.

"They'll be there any minute. Meanwhile, just hang with me. Try to stay calm."

Calm. I can't be calm. I may never be calm again.

The operator kept asking questions, and Laura guessed she answered them correctly. Her mind was on the shooting. But she figured part of the procedure was for the operator to keep her on the line until the police arrived.

Just when she thought no one would ever come, she heard a pounding on the door. "Police. Open up."

"The patrolmen are here," Laura said to the operator. She heard a voice on the other end of the line, but she ignored it and ended the call. Help was at hand. She hurried to the front door.

After a quick peek through the side window to confirm that it was indeed a policeman on her porch, Laura opened the door. "Ma'am, please step back away from the doorway," the officer said. He reached up and turned off the porch light. "Let's get you inside and keep you safe."

The uniformed patrolman standing in her foyer looked like he'd just stepped out of a recruiting poster—if not for the police, then for the Marines. Laura estimated his height at an inch or two over six feet, and his build was athletic, to say the least. He removed his billed cap and hit it against his leg a couple of times to knock off the snow. His red hair was cut short, a military style she'd heard called "high and tight."

Before he could say anything, she heard a car stop outside. The policeman opened the door wide enough to look out, and Laura edged up beside him to see another police cruiser pulling up and parking beside the one already sitting at the curb. The officer who emerged differed from the man who stood beside Laura in several respects: shorter, more compact, female, and black. But she strode up the walk with one hand on her holstered weapon, exuding the vibe of "I'll take care of this"—a true policeman's attitude.

"That's Officer Woodard. I'm Officer Briggs," the first policeman said.

At the door, Briggs looked at the newcomer and said, "Woodard, there've been no more shots since the call, but I haven't checked outside."

"I'll do that," Woodard said. "You take care of things in here." She took a five-cell Maglite from a loop on her belt and started walking away, one hand still on her pistol.

Briggs closed the door. "Tell me what happened."

Laura tried to give her story the same way she would present a case at a medical conference—no wasted words, just the facts of the matter. She had to stop a few times and gather herself when the enormity of what had just happened hit her, but she was eventually able to describe the events of the shooting. "You may want to check with Sergeant Fuller," she concluded. "He's investigating the apparent murder of my aunt, and this could be connected."

Could be? There's no could be about it. It's got to be connected. First they try to kill me with a car, then they shoot at me. Someone doesn't want me to have my share of Aunt Ina's money.

Briggs nodded. "I'll call him before I leave, and he'll get a copy of my report. Now, where were you when the shooting took place?"

Laura took Briggs into the living room. Cold wind came through the shattered window, billowing the drapes. The policeman turned on the lights and pointed to two bullet holes at about head height on the wall opposite the shattered window. "That's where the bullets hit. I'll call a crime scene tech before I leave, and she'll dig those out."

"Will they help identify the shooter?"

"If the slugs aren't too misshapen, we can compare the markings on them with test shots from a weapon, but only if we have a gun to check," Briggs said. "The slugs themselves won't tell us much."

Laura wiped away a trickle of blood from her neck. "Is it okay if I tend to these cuts now?"

"Do you want the EMTs?" Briggs asked. "I can have them here in just a few minutes."

"No, I'm a physician. I can take care of it." She pointed to the hallway. "I'll be in the bathroom if you need me."

Laura went into the downstairs half-bath, just off the hall. Working with tweezers and a hand mirror she found in a cabinet drawer, she carefully removed several glass shards from her neck and face. None of the scrapes and superficial cuts on her hands and knees had glass in them, and by this time the bleeding had almost stopped. She washed her head, face, legs, and hands with soap and water. After drying them, she applied antibiotic ointment to the areas where the glass had penetrated. She decided against adhesive bandages. *They probably wouldn't stick anyway.*

When Laura emerged, she saw Officer Woodard coming through the front door. "It's all clear out there," she said. "And if there were any footprints or tire tracks, the snow has already covered them."

The same way the snow covered the tracks in Aunt Ina's yard. "Thank you for checking," Laura said.

Laura heard the garage door go up. "That will be my husband," she said.

Briggs nodded and started toward the door that led from the garage into the kitchen, his hand hovering over his weapon.

Laura had thought about phoning Carter after the shooting, but it was more important to get the police here. Besides, she knew he would be focused on whatever medical problem caused him to be called out. She had planned to break the news of the shooting to him when he got back, but apparently the police had other ideas.

As Carter came through the door, Briggs looked meaningfully at the other police officer.

Woodard nodded. "Ma'am, can we go to another room— maybe your bedroom? I'll want to go over your story one more time." The officer gently herded Laura toward the stairs.

Laura doubted that one more recitation of her story would help, but apparently Briggs wanted to talk with Carter alone. Surely he wasn't a suspect. Then she had a disturbing thought. Would he get her share of Aunt Ina's money if Laura were dead? She should check into that. But was there anyone she could trust with her question?

Another thought crossed her mind. Was it possible Carter wanted her out of the way so he could be with someone else?

Mitzi's name came unbidden to her mind. Laura pressed her fingertips against her temples and pushed, as though she could banish such thoughts. When would this nightmare end?

Carter called up the stairs, "Laura, I've finished talking with Officer Briggs. You can come down now."

They met at the foot of the stairway and hugged. She held him tightly for what seemed like a long time. When Laura finally turned Carter loose, he said, "Are you okay?"

"I'm fine. Just a little scared."

"I still think you need a pistol," Carter said. Then he saw Briggs coming their way. "We'll talk later."

"I have a couple of phone calls to make," Briggs said, taking out his cell phone.

"We'll wait in the kitchen," Laura said.

"No need. You can stay here. There's nothing private about this." First, he talked with someone he referred to as a crime scene tech. Then he phoned Sergeant Fuller. After ending that call, he turned to Laura and Carter, who were still standing near him in the hall. "The sergeant says so long as you're safe tonight, he'll talk with you soon, probably tomorrow. Patsy Sawyer, the crime scene tech, is on her way. She shouldn't be here very long."

"Thanks for responding so quickly," Carter said. "I know your presence meant a lot to my wife."

"Just doing my job," Briggs said. "As soon as Patsy is finished, I'd suggest you block that window with plywood or plastic sheeting. And I'm going to ask the dispatcher to have a car keep an eye on your house until morning."

"Thank you," Laura said. "Carter and I haven't discussed it, but we may be getting an alarm system."

Carter looked at his wife. "I don't mind getting one, but it won't protect you from another shooting from outside."

"No," Laura said. "But it will keep people out of the house. And I'll feel more secure."

Woodard was the first officer to leave. Briggs waited to introduce Patsy to the homeowners before he left. While the crime scene tech took pictures of the living room, then dug out the two slugs, Carter inclined his head toward the kitchen, and his wife followed him there.

"Now are you ready to have a gun for protection?" he asked Laura.

"I'm tempted," Laura said. "But it would take some time to buy one, get a permit, and take classes in how to use it."

Carter reached into the right-hand pocket of his sport coat and pulled out a pistol. "This is a .38-caliber revolver. I've had it since shortly after starting to practice here. I have a permit and everything. I've been keeping it in the glove compartment of my car for nights when I have to go out on a call. But maybe now would be a good time to have it in the house."

He could see that Laura was torn. Part of her wanted the security of having a gun on the premises. But her innate dislike for firearms was also evident. "Why don't we put it in the drawer of the entryway table?" she said.

"Would you use it?" Carter asked.

"If I have to."

At that moment, they heard the garage door go up again. In a few moments, Zack walked through the door into the kitchen. He held a large plastic bag bearing the Walmart logo, with what appeared to be part of a green cable-knit sweater peeking out of the sack.

"Zack, someone just shot through the front window and almost killed me," Laura said.

Zack seemed to take a minute to process the news. Then he shook his head. "Wow. Are you okay?"

"I'm okay," Laura said. "Just shaken. Is the snow getting heavier out there?"

"Some," Zack said. "But that's not the big news."

"What do you mean?" Carter asked.

"After I bought these clothes, as I was walking across the parking lot, a dark sedan almost ran me over." Zack shook his head. "At first I thought maybe they'd skidded on some ice and snow, but the car seemed to be under control throughout the whole thing. I think . . . I think whoever was driving was trying to kill me."

Adela Reyes was drying her hair when her cell phone vibrated in the pocket of her jeans. She shut off the hair dryer and laid it aside while she answered the call. "Hello?"

"Adela? This is Terry Briggs. Did I call at a bad time?"

"Not at all," she said. "Just celebrating this first day of the year by cleaning up around my apartment, then washing my hair. What's up?"

"I'm working the mid-shift tonight, and I had a call that seems to intersect the case you're working with Sergeant Fuller."

"What about it?"

She listened intently as Briggs told her about the shooting at the home of Dr. Laura Morris. "I've already reported this to Sergeant Fuller, but I thought I'd let you know too. I don't know if he'll want to go out tonight to talk with Dr. Morris, but you could casually give him a call to ask him if there's anything new on the case."

"And if he says there is, I can volunteer to go with him." She ran her fingers through her dark hair and decided it was dry enough. Besides, she usually just pulled it into a ponytail because of the uniform cap she wore. "Thanks, Terry. I owe you one."

"Well, if you really feel that way, how about dinner or a movie . . . or maybe both? If you can fit it into your schedule."

She was pretty certain Briggs had been on the brink of asking her out before but stopped short. Was he afraid to engage in fraternization in front of Fuller? She had a hard time imagining that Terry Briggs was afraid of anything.

Maybe it was easier for him to do it on the phone rather than in person. What he didn't know was that she'd been waiting for him to get up his nerve and ask her, so this was a definite win-win situation for both of them. "Sounds great, Terry, but it will have to be after this case winds up. You won't forget?"

"No chance of that," Briggs said.

Jason Fuller hung up his phone and turned toward his wife, who was giving him the "what was that?" look. "Which call are you curious about?" he asked.

"From what I could tell," Lily said, "they were both about the same thing. Are you going to have to go out tonight?" They were sitting in front of a fire in their living room, and as she spoke, she looked at the snow falling outside the window.

"No, there's nothing I need to do right now. I just have to do a bit of thinking—outside the box."

"About the case of the woman found in the snow outside her house?"

He nodded. "We've searched high and low without turning up a will, so the laws of the state of Texas determine who will inherit. We've looked at the three people who stand to benefit, as well as the spouses of the two who are married, and they're all in the clear for the night that woman was found. Of course, they could have paid someone to do it, but these don't seem to be the kind of people who would have access to a person like that."

"So where does that leave you?"

"I'm not sure." He sat for a few moments, then a grin spread over his face.

"Why are you smiling?" his wife asked.

"Because I just realized I might have been asking the wrong question."

"What's the right one?" Lily asked.

"Why was the woman's body left outside in the snow?"

7

When Dr. Laura Morris had a lot on her plate, she did what she was doing now—she made a list. This Saturday, January 2, she was thinking of the calls she needed to make, first categorizing them according to their importance and whether the offices involved would be open today, then making her list accordingly. She was trying to figure out if she'd be able to reach the Tarrant County Medical Examiner's office today, when the doorbell interrupted her. Sighing, she shoved her list aside, took one more sip from the coffee cup in front of her, and pushed back from her kitchen table.

When she peeked outside, she saw Fay Autrey standing on the porch. Laura wondered what brought her aunt's neighbor here today. Visiting with this woman certainly wasn't on the list she was making, but Laura couldn't leave her standing on the porch. The cold weather was turning Ms. Autrey's breath into small white clouds, and last night's snow covered the yard and sidewalk. Laura opened the door. "Come in out of the cold."

Ms. Autrey stamped her feet a couple of times on the porch to get rid of the snow on them before coming into the house. She rubbed her gloved hands together, then removed the gloves and shoved them into the pocket of her coat.

"I'd invite you into the living room, but . . . we had an accident there last night. Carter blocked the broken window with plywood, but it's still cold in that room, so I'm keeping it shut off." *And I don't want to invite you into the kitchen. You'd settle in with a cup of coffee and stay most of the morning, and I have things to do.*

"No problem," Ms. Autrey said. "Where are the others?"

"Carter went back to the hospital for a bit. And Zack's still asleep," Laura said. "So, what can I do for you?"

"I was wondering about your aunt's car."

"What about it?" Was this something else that would need her attention?

"I used my car for over a year to run errands for Ina," Ms. Autrey said. "It has quite a few miles on it, and I can't afford the repairs it needs. On the other hand, there's a nice low-mileage Chrysler sitting in your aunt's garage. I started it up for her once a week to keep the battery charged. I drove it around the block every month or so. Now I was hoping you'd sell it to me."

Or give it to you. Well, Laura wasn't going to make that decision right now. Besides, she still wasn't sure she had the authority to handle her aunt's estate to that extent. "I'll keep it in mind, Ms. Autrey. It's much too early to make those decisions, but we'll let you know." And, trying not to be too obvious about it, Laura had the woman out the front door in a few more minutes.

She was halfway to the kitchen table when she heard the garage door. In a few moments, Carter came in and headed straight for the coffeepot.

"How's your patient?" Laura asked.

"Doing well," Carter said, pouring himself a cup. "Patients who've undergone laparoscopic appendectomies have a lot less pain. I've got him up and walking today. He should be able to go home on Monday."

He seated himself next to her at the kitchen table and gestured toward the pad and pencil in front of her. "Making one of your lists?"

"It appears to be up to me to make final arrangements for Aunt Ina. I've got to find out when the medical examiner will release the body, call a funeral director, arrange for a church service and burial—"

"Take it easy," Carter said. "You don't have to do all that right now. Drink your coffee. I want to talk about what you plan to do with Zack."

Laura sipped from her cup. "What do you mean?"

"I mean he can't stay here indefinitely. He didn't offer to give me back any change from the money I gave him for clothes, but that's okay. He's your brother. I plan to get him a suit, dress shirt, tie, and nice shoes for Aunt Ina's funeral. Again, I don't mind spending the money. But I want to know what his plans are."

"His plans." She made it a statement, not a question.

"Yes. If he thinks he's going to live here rent-free, sleeping until noon, using one of our cars, he needs to know there's an expiration date on our kindness." Carter drank half the coffee left in his cup in two big gulps. "Sorry, maybe I shouldn't say anything. But, brother or not, there's just something funny about the way he showed up as soon as there was money to be had."

"Talking about me?" Zack stood in the doorway. His blond hair was tousled. The T-shirt and sweatpants in which he'd slept were wrinkled. His bare feet were encased in grimy athletic socks that had probably at one time been white.

"Just talking about what we need to do over the next few days," Laura said. "Help yourself to the coffee. And what would you like me to fix you for breakfast?"

Sergeant Fuller thought the squad room would be empty when he walked in on Saturday morning. Instead, he saw Adela Reyes sitting at the same desk she'd been using for the past three days. "I didn't expect to see you here today," he said, hanging his coat on the back of his chair.

"When we talked last night, you said there was no need to go out, that we'd follow up the shooting at Dr. Morris's house this morning." She spread her hands. "Well, it's this morning. And since I'm a part of this team, here I am."

Fuller extracted some notes from his coat pocket, then pulled out his chair and sat. He booted up his computer, and without looking up from the screen said, "Funny how your call last night came right after the notification I got from Officer Briggs. You wouldn't have the word out that you want to hear anything that might pertain to this case, would you? I mean, that's all supposed to go to me."

"No sir. I'd never do that."

"Good," Fuller said. Then he smiled. "But I sort of noticed that Terry Briggs has had his eye on you. If he wanted to get on your good side, I don't think anyone would expect you to turn down a call with information. You wouldn't, would you?"

"No sir—I mean, Sergeant," Reyes said. "Now, what do you have for me to do?"

Laura and Carter sat down to a late lunch of sandwiches. "Would you like to bless it?" she said.

Carter nodded and offered a brief prayer over the food.

Laura knew from long experience that Carter's prayers were always short and to the point. Sometimes she wondered about their sincerity, but in his quiet way Carter seemed to have a good relationship with the Lord. Maybe he brought his surgeon's mentality to the activity of praying. Decide what you wanted to say, say it, and move on.

Carter picked up the mug of tomato soup that accompanied his sandwich. He sipped without a change in his expression. Hot liquids never seemed to bother him.

"So how's the list coming?" he asked.

"The medical examiner will release Aunt Ina's body this morning. I've contacted Mulkey-Mason Funeral Directors, and they'll do the pickup and preparation. There wasn't anyone at the church, but I reached the minister on call at home, and we've tentatively set the service for Tuesday morning."

"You've been busy," Carter said around a mouthful of grilled cheese sandwich.

"Not busy enough," Laura said. "We still have to decide on hymns, arrange for pallbearers, check on Aunt Ina's cemetery plot. But it's coming together."

Carter reached over and put his hand over Laura's. "I know you're the one holding everything together, getting it all done, but let me help if I can."

"Well, other than watching my back, since someone is apparently trying to kill me, I can't think of anything you can do," Laura said. "I don't mind doing this for Aunt Ina. But what gets me, what I can't shake and what we're all ignoring, is the elephant in the room."

"You mean—"

"That's right. She didn't die a natural death. And the person who murdered her might be someone in our own family," Laura said.

"What are you all in such earnest conversation about?" Zack stood in the door. He wore new-looking jeans and a sweatshirt.

Laura looked at Carter and gave her head a minimal shake. "Nothing, Zack. Come on in and sit down. Would you like some lunch?"

The closed door to the drafty living room muted the ringing of the phone. Carter rose from the table. "I'll get it. It may be the glass company. I asked them to replace that window as soon as possible, and they were going to call me back when they were on their way."

Zack yawned, then sat down at the kitchen table.

"Still tired?" Laura asked him.

"Yeah, I'm afraid I haven't recovered from the bus trip. And, of course, someone tried to run me down last night." He grimaced. "That's probably got something to do with why I'm having trouble sleeping soundly."

Carter came back into the kitchen shaking his head.

"I take it that wasn't the glass company," Laura said.

"No, I guess they'll call soon."

Zack rose at about the same time as Carter sat back down. "You know, I'm not hungry. I think I'll go back to my room and try on the other clothes I bought."

When Zack was gone, Laura said, "Well, what was the phone call about? The conversation was too long for a wrong number. Was it the hospital? Or your service?"

Carter was quiet for a moment. "It was Mitzi. She wanted to know if there was anything she could do."

"I guess she's trying to help, but I wish she'd stop calling so much," Laura said. "I've told her we have it under control, but she still calls once or twice a day anyway." She looked at Carter. "Was that all?"

"No, I got a cell phone call right after I hung up with Mitzi. One of my patients has spiked a fever. I'll be back soon." He bent over the table to kiss Laura, grabbed his coat, and went out the door into the garage.

First a phone call from an attractive family friend, then her husband rushes away. Laura decided that, if she were the suspicious type, she'd start worrying about now. Then again, she had enough to worry about without adding to it.

"I've made those calls you wanted," Adela Reyes said. "Here's what I found out." She passed several pages from a yellow legal pad to Sergeant Fuller.

Fuller adjusted his reading glasses and studied what Reyes had written. What he had was actually a series of calendars for the dates of December 25 through December 30. Each one was headed with the name of a different person, and in the date boxes she'd written the activities and location of each individual. For instance, the box for Zack Morris showed that he was in Las Vegas from December 25 until midday on December 30. Then he was on a series of three busses on December 31 and January 1.

"Did Robert and Claudia Morris complain much?" Fuller asked.

"Claudia didn't seem to find anything unusual about my asking. Robert, on the other hand—well, he gave me the usual lawyer talk about invasion of privacy, mixed with 'I don't see the relevance,' but he gave me the information I wanted."

"And?"

"Robert and his wife say they didn't have any contact with Ms. Patrick from before Christmas until she was found dead.

It looks like, other than his time spent with clients or working in his office, he was with his wife at one social function or another."

"And I checked the corroborating witnesses for both of them. His story holds up. There are some holes in hers, but then again, I don't guess that's unusual."

"How about the two doctors: Laura Morris and her husband, Carter Hawkins?"

"They've got some holes as well, but none that just stand out. We know that Dr. Morris and her husband were with Ina Bell Patrick on Christmas day, and she called her aunt on December twenty-sixth."

"Okay," Fuller said. "Here's one more story to check on. And while you make the call, let me see those phone records."

"Is there a reason you're going back and checking alibis for several days before Ms. Patrick was found?"

"You have as much information as I do," Fuller said. "Let me know when you figure it out."

Laura cleaned up the lunch dishes, then sat down at her kitchen table to start working on her list again. Occasionally her thoughts would drift to the new window in the living room. Although Carter had wanted to consider replacing the shattered pane with bulletproof glass, she'd managed to talk him out of it. "Once this is over, no one's going to be shooting at either of us," she'd told him. So the company was installing plain glass, slightly tinted to filter the afternoon sun.

Carter came up behind Laura, hugged her, and kissed her hair. "How're you doing?"

"Other than the fact that my aunt has been murdered, and it's likely that the murderer might be a member of my family—just swell," she said.

"Heard from the police?"

"Not today," she said. "I did talk with Robert for a minute after lunch, though. He asked that same question. Do you think he's anxious for them to find Aunt Ina's killer?"

"No, I think Robert wants this to be over so he can get his share of Aunt Ina's money," Carter said.

She chewed for a moment on the eraser of the pencil she held. "I guess the police have checked everyone's background as part of their investigation. Maybe Robert is fishing to see if the police have mentioned what they found out about Claudia."

"Probably," Carter said. "They haven't mentioned it, but if we could find it out, I have no doubt the police could, as well."

"Do you think that Robert or Claudia might be so desperate for more money that they'd murder Aunt Ina?" Laura asked.

"If so, I'm sure the police will discover that too." Carter got a Dr Pepper from the refrigerator and flipped the can open.

"Why does he stay with Claudia?" Laura asked.

"In my opinion, my brother-in-law is in a bad marriage, but he's staying in it because the benefits outweigh the bad parts . . . for both of them."

The ringing of the phone made both Laura and Carter look up. "I'll get it," he said.

In a moment he was back, holding the portable phone against his chest to mute what he was saying. "It's Officer Reyes. She wants to know if Zack is here."

"He's still in his room," Laura said. "Should I get him?"

Carter relayed that information, listened for a moment, then said, "Sure. Thanks for calling."

"What was that about?" Laura asked.

"She said we should call them as soon as Zack came downstairs. They want to come by and talk with him, but in the meantime they have someone else to see."

"I wonder if they have some more questions for him," Laura said.

"I don't know," Carter replied. "But she sounded serious. She said to call them and not let him leave the house."

Fay Autrey looked around her and shook her head. The house was clean, but the rugs were threadbare, and the furniture was beginning to show signs of wear. There was a TV set in the living room, but it wasn't one of the big-screen models. The kitchen countertops were laminate, not marble or quartz. The range and refrigerator were serviceable but had seen better days.

She and her late husband had never had much money. The proceeds from his insurance hadn't gone far, so she was happy when Ina asked for her help. Fay was glad to run errands and do "favors" for her neighbor in hopes there'd be something in it for her—if not now, then certainly after Ina Bell died. But when was that going to happen?

Her neighbor was dead. Fay had looked high and low in Ina Bell's house but found no trace of a will. Without one, the estate would be divided among the woman's closest kin. That would freeze Fay out. She grinned at the pun. No, however it went down, she was going to get some money. It was just a matter of when and how.

She was about to wash the dishes in her sink, when she heard a pounding on the door. Her doorbell only worked about half the time, so maybe it was just someone knocking who'd gotten tired of pushing the button. Then she heard it—a loud voice, coming through clearly. "Fay Autrey, this is the police. Open the door."

Fay stood transfixed for a moment. She had to open the door, but maybe she could delay them for a bit. She stepped back into her bedroom and called through the open doors into the hall and living room. "I've just gotten out of the shower."

Another knock, just as loud as the first. "We'll give you five minutes to open this door—starting now."

Fay opened a drawer and pulled out a cell phone hidden under some linens. It only had one number in the favorites list, and her finger stabbed at it. The call was answered on the third ring.

"What is it? You know you're not supposed to call me on this cell unless it's an emergency."

"This may be one."

"Hang on. I need to make sure no one can hear me." Various noises followed, including the closing of a door. "Okay, I can talk, but make it quick."

"There are police at my door. I've put them off for a minute or two. Have you heard anything about it?"

"No."

"Do you think—?"

"Hush. If we run right now, we'll lose any chance we might have. Just stick to your story, and I'll stick to mine. Now hang up."

The banging at the door was back. Fay hurried to the shower and stuck her head inside long enough to get it wet.

Then she quickly ran a towel over her hair before wrapping it turban-style around her head. "I'm coming."

When she got to the door, she opened it and said, "Sergeant Fuller. Officer Reyes. Didn't the doorbell work?"

Laura stood at the living room window and watched the glass-repair van pull away from her house. The workers had done a nice job with the installation, including cleaning up evidence of their presence. In a few minutes, she'd vacuum the carpet, sofa, and any other areas where tiny spicules of glass could be hiding. The central heating system was already working to combat the chill that had settled over the room from the damaged window. Everything looked like it was back to normal. But Laura knew better.

Nothing was normal anymore. Not only was her mother's only living relative dead but the police were certain Aunt Ina been murdered. Laura had been willing to try to forget almost being run over in the hospital parking lot, but the broken window was a tangible reminder that someone had tried to kill her as well. And that someone was still out there—waiting for another chance.

"Hey, Sis. I think I'm going to go out for a while." Zack stood in the doorway. The ragged fatigue jacket had been replaced by a new coat, which he wore over a flannel shirt and jeans. It appeared he'd made an attempt to comb his hair, although tufts of it still stuck up at random. It looked as if he'd tried to shave with the disposable razor she kept in the bathroom adjoining the guest room, but she could tell he'd missed a couple of areas. And the lack of a beard simply drew even more attention to the scar on his face.

Zack's story was that he'd turned his life around. He'd come back home. He was saying and doing the right things. He'd even made an effort to look more presentable. If all that was true, why did she feel ill at ease around her brother?

"Zack, Officer Reyes asked me to call the police station as soon as you woke up," Laura said. "I'm certain they want to talk with you some more. Actually, they said not to let you leave."

"I'll be right back, and then you can call them," he said. "But for now, could I borrow your car? I'm supposed to pick up some clothes I bought at Dillard's. The alterations should be done by now, and I really need those pants."

"I think you should stay here and let me make the call first," she said.

Zack frowned. "Look, Sis. I'm twenty-seven years old. I've been out on my own for a while. Why not let me handle this? I'll only be gone for a few minutes. Then you can call the police. It's probably nothing."

Laura sighed. There seemed to be no use in arguing. She walked to where she'd left her purse, dug in it to find the keys, and tossed them to him. "Be careful," she said. *I haven't said that to him since he was a kid. I wonder why it just came out now.* "And hurry back."

Sergeant Fuller looked from Fay Autrey's door to his watch to the door again. "I'll give her one more minute," he said to Reyes. "Then I'm going to plant my shoe—"

He didn't finish the sentence. The door opened and Fay Autrey stood there. She had a towel wrapped around her head but otherwise was fully dressed, wearing a clean but worn housedress and a pair of run-down tennis shoes.

"Sergeant Fuller. Officer Reyes," she said. "Didn't the doorbell work? I'm sorry you had to pound so hard to get my attention." Autrey stepped aside and waved them inside with a gesture a maître d' might use in a nice restaurant.

"Is there somewhere we can talk?" Fuller asked.

"Of course," Autrey said. She led them into her living room and pointed to a couch covered with worn tapestry-like fabric. "What can I do for you?"

"We won't need to sit down—and neither will you. Fay Autrey, you're under arrest for your role in the homicide of Ina Bell Patrick."

Reyes spun the woman around and had her hands cuffed behind her before Autrey could speak.

"I . . . I don't understand. What's this about?" Autrey said. "There must be some mistake."

Reyes started reciting. "Fay Autrey, you have the right to remain silent. Anything you say can and will be used against you. You have the right to an attorney . . ."

8

Carter came through the door from the garage into the kitchen. "It's still cold out there, but I think the snow's letting up." He moved to the counter and poured a cup of coffee.

Laura looked up from the sheet of cookies she was preparing to shovel off the baking sheet into the cookie jar. "Everything okay at the hospital? You left here in sort of a hurry after that phone call."

Carter came up behind Laura and put one arm around her, holding his cup away from her with the other. "Nothing important. Just a post-op patient with a fever." He reached down to snatch a cookie from the sheet and popped it into his mouth. "Why are you making cookies?"

"Because it's something I can do. Otherwise, I'd just be sitting on a chair somewhere, worrying. At least this keeps me busy—and it's productive, sort of." She looked up at him. "Why do you think the patient is running a fever?"

"I think he's getting an upper respiratory infection. No sign of complications from the appendectomy, but his throat's a bit raw. I ordered a throat culture and a blood count."

"Why didn't you ask—?" She stopped abruptly.

"Since it was Johnny Rivers, and you are his family doctor, I figured I'd go ahead and order what you would. I can check the results when I make rounds tomorrow." He took another warm cookie off the cookie sheet and popped it into his mouth. "Well, I'll agree with you about one thing—making cookies is certainly something you can do. And yes, it is productive."

"I'm glad you like them, because if Sergeant Fuller doesn't arrest the person who murdered Aunt Ina soon, we're going to be up to our eyeballs in cookies."

They had just booked Fay Autrey into jail. "Now we go after the other half of the team?" Reyes said as they exited the front door of the police station.

"Right," Fuller said.

As she walked toward the car, Reyes asked, "Think the arrest will hold up?"

"I ran everything we had by the district attorney," Fuller said. "It should hold together, especially after she's questioned. Besides that, as soon as we pick up her accomplice, one or the other of them is going to realize the first rule of arrested criminals—first one to rat out the other gets the best deal."

"Want to go over it with me one more time?" Reyes asked.

Fuller opened the door of the car and slid behind the wheel. "Let's talk in the car," he said. "I don't want to wait too long. The bird may already have flown—although I doubt we'll have much trouble picking him up if he has."

They both buckled in. Fuller started the car and pulled away from the police station. "It began when I thought about establishing Ms. Patrick's time of death," he said. "It was totally dependent on Autrey's story of having dinner with her the night before her body was found. If we put aside that story, Laura Morris said she'd talked with her aunt on the day after Christmas, three and a half days before her body was found. And, if we assume Ms. Patrick died later that day, everything changes. So I turned the investigation in a different direction."

"And eventually you put it together by asking—"

"Why was Ina Bell Patrick's body left in the snow? Not only was the time of death difficult to determine because her body was frozen, but the autopsy had to be delayed until the corpse thawed. When the pathologist found evidence of trauma to Ms. Patrick's head, you and I went back to Ms. Patrick's home and looked more carefully. There was no blood—the pathologist told me there was none around the contusion on her skull—but there was one brick from the fireplace that was loose. And that led me to put together a different scenario."

"Suppose Ms. Patrick died several days before her body was found, probably on the night of December twenty-sixth," Reyes said.

"Right. She and Autrey were together, perhaps having an evening meal, when Fay Autrey brought up her desire to be paid for the errands she ran for Ms. Patrick. When Patrick turned down the idea, Autrey got angry and pushed her. Ms. Patrick fell back, hitting her skull on the bricks. Maybe Autrey thought she was just stunned, but Patrick didn't wake up— instead, in just a matter of minutes, she died. "

"And Autrey didn't know what to do."

"That's when the phone at Ms. Patrick's home rang," Fuller said. "The caller ID showed it was from Las Vegas—from the number at Zack's rooming house. Ms. Autrey picked up the phone. Maybe Zack could tell her what to do about the dead woman. But it wasn't Zack. It was his roommate, calling to tell Ms. Patrick that Zack was in the hospital, and to ask if she'd guarantee his bill. That's when Ms. Autrey decided to use the incident to get her hands on some of Ina Bell Patrick's money."

"I think it was clever what she came up with," Reyes said.

"The story Zack gave his family was that he went to Las Vegas, wasted his inheritance, hit rock bottom, then discovered a ministry that helped him get back on the right course with his life. That much was true. But, as we know—based on some phone calls to the police in Las Vegas and a bit of investigating on their part— the real Zack Morris is currently in Sunrise Hospital in Las Vegas. He's recovering from two operations performed after he sustained multiple stab wounds and a fracture while trying to break up a fight between two men outside a bar on the Strip."

"Which means the Zack Morris who showed up at the sister's door was a phony."

"Right," Fuller said. "Autrey conspired with Zack's roommate to have him come here, impersonate Zack, stick around long enough to establish his right to a share of the inheritance, then disappear—but not before arranging to split the money with her. But she realized he'd have to wait a few days before traveling here."

"And that was the reason Patrick's time of death had to be delayed," Reyes said.

"The roommate had Zack's ID, but there was something else that could prove his identity even more conclusively— something Ms. Patrick had mentioned to Autrey, and that the roommate also knew. Zack had tattoos around his upper arms. The impersonator had to get those, but Autrey thought he should wait a few days after getting them, so they wouldn't look so fresh."

"When did you think of checking Autrey's phone records?" Reyes asked.

"I should have done it sooner. I found that, on the morning of December thirtieth, she called the phone at Zack's rooming house."

"Won't she claim the call was to let him know about his aunt's death?"

"She might, but I figure it was to tell Zack's roommate to get on a bus for Hilton. We checked bus company records, and they show that someone using Zack's name rode three busses to get here from Las Vegas. He used Zack's ID, but it wasn't Zack."

"No, it took a little digging, but we know who it really was."

"It was Autrey's nephew, Bud Reiger. She'd suggested him as a roommate for Zack when Ms. Patrick told her about the situation in Las Vegas. Of course, Autrey had no idea this was going to come up, but when it did, she took advantage of it."

"What about the resemblance to Zack?" Reyes asked.

"Reiger looked a bit like Zack, and with the knowledge he'd picked up from his roommate, plus a little coaching from Autrey, they thought he could pull it off. He could explain the weight loss and any failure to remember stuff by his history of drug usage. And the old scar would draw attention away from his face—people wouldn't want to stare at it."

"And when he got his share of the estate, he'd split the money with Autrey," Reyes said.

"He planned to stick around just long enough for Ms. Patrick's estate to go to probate. Then he'd arrange for his share of the money to go to a bank somewhere, and disappear."

"It was simple how Ms. Autrey delayed the discovery of Ina Bell Patrick's body," Reyes said.

"By putting her body in the chest freezer Ms. Patrick had in her garage? It was. But once we figured that out, we looked through the large garbage bin behind Patrick's house. It had been emptied, but we still found one box of frozen food that had stuck to the bottom—one of the boxes she removed to make room for the body."

"Didn't someone help her?" Reyes asked. "Could one woman carry the body alone?"

"Ms. Patrick was frail, and Autrey was strong despite her age. She probably had no trouble getting the body into the freezer. She might have had to let the corpse warm up to straighten her out when she was ready to put Patrick in the snow, but that was okay. She wasn't in a hurry. She'd put Patrick into the freezer right after she died, wearing the same clothes she had on at the time. But Autrey didn't stop to add a coat or shoes before dumping the body into the snow. Matter of fact, she didn't dump it. Some instinct—maybe their friendship, such as it was—made her lay out Patrick's body. That was a mistake. It made me think something was wrong about the whole scenario."

Fuller pulled the squad car to the curb and shut off the engine. "Well," he said to Reyes, "Let's go scoop up Autrey's accomplice and let the family know what's going on."

Laura and Carter sat side by side on the sofa in their living room. He was reading a book. She was thumbing through the pages of a magazine. The new window was framed by open drapes. The central heat had removed the chill caused by the open window, and the room felt cozy. Outside, the light was fading, and the porch lamp cast a soft glow on the blanket of snow covering the front yard.

The scene spoke of tranquility, but Laura's mind was anything but tranquil. Her aunt had been murdered, her family members were prime suspects, and her husband might be having an affair. No, she wasn't very tranquil right now.

She reached for the plate of cookies on the coffee table, then withdrew her hand. She wasn't really hungry. "I wonder why Zack isn't back," she said. "I told him he needed to return Officer Reyes's call, but he ignored me, took my car, and went out."

"I don't guess you could restrain him by force," Carter said. "But if he doesn't show pretty soon, I've a good mind to report your car stolen. That's no way—"

The doorbell rang. "I'll bet that's him," Laura said. "He doesn't have a key."

"No, but your car has a garage door opener."

"Maybe he had to park out front. I wouldn't be surprised if the snow had drifted in front of the garage door," Laura said.

"Since I got home? I doubt that," Carter said.

Laura peeked through the side window and her hope gave way to disappointment. It wasn't Zack. It was Sergeant Fuller, accompanied by Officer Reyes. She opened the door and ushered them in.

Once she'd taken their coats and gloves, Laura said, "We're in the living room. I told Zack you wanted to talk with him, but he borrowed my car and took off."

"I was afraid he might run, but that's okay. We had another arrest we needed to make first. This was really her scheme." He shrugged. "If you'll just give Officer Reyes the license plate number and description of your car, we'll find it—and Zack—probably within a few hours."

Laura frowned but did as Fuller asked. Reyes wrote down the information and excused herself, pulling out her cell phone as she walked away.

Fuller followed Laura into the living room and took a seat on the sofa. He nodded to acknowledge Carter's presence, but didn't speak until Reyes came back into the room. "Done," she said.

"So . . ." Laura hesitated. "It sounds like you're getting close to solving my aunt's . . . her murder. Is my brother, Zack, involved in some way?"

"Yes and no," Fuller said. "Yes and no."

Thank goodness for small blessings. The roads were passable, with no ice or significant accumulation of snow, even though white flakes continued to spit. The wipers kept the windshield clear, and there seemed to be plenty of wiper fluid for times when a passing vehicle splashed muddy snowmelt onto the car.

The gas gauge showed a bit more than half a tank. He had no idea what kind of mileage this Chevrolet Malibu would get, but that should be enough to get him down the road. The last thing he needed was to run out of gas.

He'd hoped for a few more creature comforts for the trip ahead of him, but there were no CDs in the player, and the radio presets were for either Christian stations or talk radio. Neither appealed to him. That was probably okay, though. He needed to pay attention to his driving.

It wouldn't be good to have some cop stop him for breaking a traffic law. He concentrated on keeping the car below the speed limit and obeying all the signs. Would the proper papers be in the glove compartment? He hoped so. He touched his wallet where he knew there was a driver's license. Then he realized he hadn't checked to see if it had expired. Should he pull over and look? No, it was better to keep going. He'd just be extra careful as he drove away from Hilton, Texas.

A bit of regret crossed his mind. They had almost pulled it off. At first, the scheme seemed harebrained, but as they'd refined it, it began to make more sense. For a while it seemed to be working. He didn't know how much money would eventually have been involved. Well, there was no reason to cry over spilled milk. There would be other chances. Right now he just wanted to get away, to disappear completely off the radar.

He was glad he'd played a hunch and driven by Fay Autrey's house. Despite the assurances he'd given her over the phone, he couldn't shake the bad feeling about what might be going down. And when he saw her coming out of her house in handcuffs, he knew it was time to cut his losses and run.

His thoughts had taken him away from concentrating on his driving, and he looked down to see that the speedometer had crept up to almost fifteen miles per hour over the posted speed limit. He took his foot off the accelerator, but it was too late. He glanced in his rearview mirror, and his chest tightened. He felt his throat closing up. If the flashing lights atop the black-and-white SUV behind him weren't enough to get his attention, the brief *whoop* of the siren was.

He slowed and pulled onto the shoulder of the road. As the policeman approached, he rolled down his window. "Good evening, Officer," he said to the uniformed patrolman standing outside the car. "Is there a problem?"

Laura looked puzzled. "What do you mean by 'yes and no'?"

"Let me give you the whole story before we talk about Zack," Fuller said. "To begin with, we've just arrested Fay Autrey for her role in the homicide of your aunt, Ina Bell Patrick."

"How . . . ? What . . . ? Would you explain?" Laura asked.

"Was she a suspect?"

"When a case like this starts out, everyone is a suspect," Fuller said. "We started, as we generally do, with the family members. After all, you were the ones who'd inherit Ina Bell Patrick's money."

"You suspected us?" Laura said.

"Well, you are family members," Fuller said. "And Robert Morris certainly had a motive—he and his wife could use some money. She's spending it faster than he can make it. And, according to the managing partner at his firm, he isn't going to get a bonus or raise, even though he's been doing a good job. With the money from his aunt's estate, he could set up his own law firm. The income might also be enough to satisfy his wife. It seemed like a good deal for them."

"But he didn't do it," Carter said.

"No, Robert and his wife, Claudia, had solid alibis. They were with some of Fort Worth's leading citizens when we think Ina Bell Patrick was killed."

"What about me?" Laura asked. "Did you actually check me out as well?'

"We cleared you in a hurry. Besides, you really had no motive to kill Ms. Patrick." Fuller paused and turned to Carter. "We did, however, take a longer look at you. You don't have the need for money that your brother-in-law and his wife do, but for a bit we wondered if you tried to get rid of your wife because you were having an affair."

Laura felt her heart clench. She balled her hands into fists, and stared into her lap. Were her suspicions about to be proved right?

Then Fuller shook his head. "But there was no evidence of that."

Laura felt a rush of relief mixed with shame—shame that she'd thought Carter might be cheating on her. She reached over and took his hand.

"What about Zack?" Carter asked.

"We'll get to him. Let's talk first about Fay Autrey," Fuller said. "I realized that the time of death for Ina Bell Patrick was totally dependent on Autrey's story of having dinner with her the night before her body was found. Before that, Dr. Morris said she'd talked with Ms. Patrick on the day after Christmas, three and a half days before her body was found. If we assume Ms. Patrick died later that day, everything changes."

Laura shook her head as Fuller told the story. She couldn't believe all this was happening.

"What did Autrey say?" Carter asked when Fuller got to the part where he'd arrested Autrey.

"She didn't say anything—just lawyered up."

"So what about Zack?" Laura asked.

"The story he gave you was true. That's what happened to Zack. But the man who showed up at your doorstep isn't Zack."

Laura looked puzzled. "Explain yourself."

"I made some calls to the Las Vegas police. They did some checking and reported back to me. It seems that right now, the real Zack Morris is in Sunrise Hospital in Las Vegas. He's recovering from two operations performed after he sustained multiple stab wounds and a fracture while trying to break up a fight between two men outside a bar on the Strip."

"So who is the man pretending to be Zack?" Laura asked.

"Zack's roommate, Fay Autrey's nephew. His name is Bud Reiger."

"We let him get away," Laura said.

"You couldn't have restrained him forcibly," Fuller said. "But we have the description and license plate number of your car, and I'll wager the fake Zack is going to be in custody before morning."

"What about Zack's brush with death—the car that almost ran him down?" Carter asked.

"Who can corroborate that story?" Fuller said. "No one. We only have Zack's word that it happened. Odds are that after Dr. Miller's scare with the shooting, he decided to come up with a story of his own."

"So Ms. Autrey killed Aunt Ina Bell, then hid her body until her nephew could surface and impersonate my younger brother?" Laura said. "What was her motive?"

"The oldest one in the book, and one of the first things a cop learns to look for when investigating a murder—money. It's always money."

Laura looked at Carter as the door closed behind Fuller. "What will they charge Fay Autrey with? And what about the fake Zack? What was his name? Reiger?" she asked.

"I'm not a lawyer," Carter said. "I guess if what Fuller said about the incident that killed Aunt Ina Bell is accurate, they might make the charge manslaughter. And she's probably guilty of tampering with evidence—and abuse of a corpse, although that one is most likely a misdemeanor. Of course, if they can prove their intent to defraud you out of part of the inheritance, there'd be that charge against both her and the man pretending to be Zack."

"What about Zack—I mean Reiger?" Laura asked.

"I think Fuller was right. They probably won't have too much trouble finding him. They can hold Reiger on a charge of car theft, but that's sort of iffy since you gave him the keys—although you did give them under false pretenses. There's undoubtedly some sort of charge for impersonation, and maybe fraud in there somewhere. I guess it depends on what the district attorney decides." He held his palms up. "That will be up to them. I'm just glad it's over."

Laura looked at the window. The drapes were drawn, hiding the glass that had been so recently replaced. "We don't know which one was shooting at me, but I guess the police will determine that."

"My money's on Reiger," Carter said. "I still wonder if I shouldn't have had them put in bullet-proof glass when they repaired that window."

"Don't be silly," Laura replied. "I don't plan to spend the rest of my life ducking when I hear a loud noise. If the police have caught the person who killed Aunt Ina Bell, I'm not in danger."

"Are you hungry?" Carter asked.

"Maybe a snack," Laura said. "But first—Sergeant Fuller said Zack is in a Las Vegas hospital. Do you think we could talk with someone there? If he's really turned his life around, I want to help him. And even if he hasn't, he's still my brother."

"I think Fuller said he's in Sunrise Hospital. Let's see what we can do," Carter said.

It took him ten minutes of ducking in and out of automated phone mail jail, but finally Carter succeeded in convincing the hospital operator that he was indeed a doctor, and that he needed to speak to someone about Zack Morris, a patient there.

After another prolonged wait, there was a click on the line and a man's voice said, "This is Dr. Goodrich. I'm one of the trauma surgeons here. How can I help you?"

Carter pressed the button to put the call on speaker. He explained that he and Laura were physicians and what their relationship was with Zack, then told him why they were calling. "We've just learned that he's a patient at your hospital. What can you tell us?"

"I've just got about five minutes before I have to be in the OR, but, yeah, I was part of the team that worked on him when the paramedics brought him in. He'd almost bled out from multiple stab wounds. We did a laparotomy, removed his spleen, sutured a couple of bad lacerations of his liver, eventually got the bleeding under control. I don't know how much blood we ended up giving him. Almost lost him, but he's a fighter. Then he had a pretty bad fracture of his left arm, which necessitated another surgery to pin it."

"So, is he still in ICU?"

"I think they moved him today to a regular room. He's conscious, but I'd be surprised if he's ready for discharge before the middle of next week."

"Can we talk with him?"

"I wouldn't try quite yet. He's requiring a lot of pain meds that keep him pretty well out of it most of the time. But I can ask the nurse to let him know you called."

"Please do that," Laura chimed in. "And tell him I'll be out to check on him personally sometime Wednesday. I . . . I have some things I have to take care of here first."

"Sure," Goodrich said. "I hate to ask this, but I know it's going to come up pretty soon. When he came in, we didn't get any insurance information. I know they asked him later, during one of his more lucid moments, and he said he didn't have any. Is that right?"

"We'll guarantee the bill," Carter said. "When the dust settles, Zack's going to have about a half-million dollars—maybe more. The hospital will get its money."

"And, more important, he's going to have a family again," Laura added.

In the police car, Reyes's cell phone rang. She looked at Fuller, who was driving. "Shall I take that?"

He shrugged. Reyes decided that was close enough to approval. The caller ID told her all she wanted to know, and despite the professional demeanor she tried to reflect, she couldn't help smiling. "Hello, Terry."

Terrance Briggs's voice came over the cell phone so loudly that Reyes glanced left to see if Fuller reacted to it. He kept his eyes straight ahead, but she switched the phone to her right ear to keep it a bit further from possible eavesdropping.

"Can you talk right now?" he asked.

"Sort of, if we make it fast," she said.

"I noticed that you and Sergeant Fuller brought Fay Autrey in and charged her with . . . hang on while I find the paperwork." She heard pages turning. "Here it is. She's charged with homicide in the death of Ina Bell Patrick. Think the charge will stick?"

"I'm pretty sure it will," Reyes said.

"Do you think you made points with Fuller by working with him?"

"Yes," she said. She was getting a hint of where this was going.

"Well, I'm ready to collect on the debt you owe me."

"What debt?"

Fuller looked at her, but quickly turned his attention back to the road.

"Remember when I called you with information about the case, and you said something like 'I owe you'?" Briggs said. "Well, I'm calling in the debt. How about dinner and a movie? Are you free some night next week?"

Reyes couldn't help smiling. "How about Monday night? Call me, and we'll iron out the details."

As Reyes stowed her phone, Fuller said, without turning his head, "I hope it works out with Officer Briggs."

"I don't know what you mean," Reyes said.

"If you're that dense, then there's no chance you'll ever get promoted. Maybe I shouldn't put that commendation in your personnel file after all."

"Oh no. Put it in." She paused a beat, then decided to go for it. "I guess this case is over."

"Our part of it, at least."

"Sergeant, don't you want someone working with you permanently to help you on homicides and big cases?"

"Yep," Fuller said. "I've already got someone in mind."

Reyes heart sank until she heard his next words.

"That is, unless you don't want the assignment."

After they finished the call to Las Vegas, Laura and Carter were in the kitchen, drinking coffee, each lost in thought, when the phone rang again. "Would you get that?" Laura asked.

"Sure," Carter said. He hurried into the living room to answer. The conversation was short, and when Carter returned, he said, "I've got to go out for a while."

While he was shrugging into his coat, he said, "That was the operating room. Jim Hutchison is doing an aortic aneurysm. He's in trouble and needs my help. I'll be back as soon as I can." Carter kissed Laura and headed out the door.

Laura had just about decided to go upstairs and shower, when the doorbell rang. Who could be at the door this late at night? Had Zack, or Bud, or whatever his name really was come back? Was he at the door with a gun, planning to eliminate her? Maybe the plan for him to get his share of her aunt's inheritance had blown up in his face, or maybe he just wanted revenge. Carter's revolver was in the table at the entryway. Maybe she'd grab it—but could she use it?

She flipped on the porch light and peered out the side window to identify her visitor. After only a moment's hesitation, she unlocked the door and opened it.

"Mitzi, what are you doing here so late?"

Mitzi rubbed her feet on the welcome mat, then hurried inside. Before Laura could say anything else, Mitzi said, "Is Carter gone?"

"Yes, he left a few minutes ago. But he'll be back—"

"I just wanted to be sure he's gone. By the time he gets to the hospital, discovers that phone call was a fake, and comes back here, I'll be finished and away from here."

"I don't understand," Laura said.

Mitzi withdrew her right hand from the pocket of her coat and pointed a revolver at Laura. "I suppose I have time to explain it to you before I kill you," she said.

9

Laura's first reaction was *She can't be serious.* But the gun in Mitzi's hand was quite real, and apparently so was her intention.

"Let's move into the living room."

Laura looked with regret at the closed drawer of the table where Carter's revolver lay. *So near, and yet so far.* Mitzi waved her own gun, and Laura walked slowly into the living room.

"I want this to look like you discovered a burglary in progress, tried to stop it, and were shot." Mitzi looked around the room. "The drapes are closed. That's good. Now stand over there."

"Wait! Mitzi, what's this about? You're our friend—my friend. We stood by you during your divorce. What's gotten into you?"

"You never caught on, did you? Carter doesn't deserve you. He deserves me. I won't spend all day at my profession, like you do. I won't be comparing my career with his or compete with him. I'll clean the house and have a hot meal ready for him when he comes in. I'll be a full-time wife and mother—something you can't be."

"Mother?"

"I know you've tried without success to have children. You told me once the doctor said the fault lies with you. Well, I've had one child—true, my husband got custody of him when we divorced, but I'm not barren like you are." Tears started to streak down Mitzi's cheeks. "Carter deserves me, not you. And with you out of the picture, his way will be clear to marry me."

"So those phone calls—"

"I've tried calling his cell phone, but he doesn't answer me anymore. And half the time when I called the home phone, you answered, so I had to pretend to be just a well-meaning friend."

Laura looked at the revolver Mitzi held. "That's a .38-caliber gun, isn't it?"

"Aren't you the smart one?" Mitzi said. "Yes. My husband bought it for me right after we were married. He said it wasn't much good at a distance, and I found that out when I tried to shoot you through the window. It's what he called a 'belly gun.' He told me to get close and aim for the center of the body mass. So that's what I'll do this time."

"Why—?"

"Enough!" Mitzi said. "I know what you're doing. You want to keep me talking until Carter comes back home, but by that time I'll be gone, and you'll be dead."

What did a loaded pistol weigh—maybe a couple of pounds? Laura was hoping Mitzi would get tired of holding the gun, but her hand didn't appear to be wavering. And Mitzi's finger was on the trigger of the gun. Laura didn't know if the revolver had a safety, but if it did, Mitzi probably had taken care of that. She seemed to know what she was doing.

"Over there by that coffee table should be about right."

This was really happening. Mitzi was going to kill her. Laura felt her bowels about to loosen. The phone was too far away for Laura to grab it. The neighbors on either side were gone for the holidays, and there was no one nearby to hear a scream. It was hopeless. Was she ready to die? Not without a fight.

There might be one chance, but it was a slim one. Then again, if she didn't try, there was no chance at all.

"Can I at least pray?" Laura asked.

Mitzi laughed. "Why not? Just make it fast."

Laura bowed her head, but kept her eyes open as she confirmed the position on the coffee table of what she'd need. She took a deep breath, then in one motion scooped the big family Bible she'd saved from her parents' home and flung it as hard as possible at Mitzi, hoping to hit the woman or at least spoil her aim. Laura heard a shot, felt something hot go over her left shoulder, but by this time she was in midair, aimed at Mitzi like a heat-seeking missile.

Laura hoped her tackle would jar the gun out of Mitzi's hand, but that didn't happen. There was a loud noise, and Laura's right ear went deaf, the ambient sound replaced by a loud ringing. How many more shots did the gun hold? Wrestling wasn't going to do any good, and eventually one of those shots would hit home.

Laura wasn't a fighter, but she was desperate. She drew back her fist and launched a punch at Mitzi's chin that snapped her head back. Still holding the gun, Mitzi fell back like a robot whose power button had been turned off. Laura waited a second, but Mitzi didn't move. Was she playing possum?

Rather than pick up the gun, Laura half-rose and kicked at Mitzi's hand until the pistol skittered a couple of yards away. Still unsure whether Mitzi was fully out of action, Laura bent over her and lifted the woman's eyelid. The eyeball was rolled upward, and there was no reaction when Laura touched the white part of the eye. Mitzi was unconscious—at least, for now.

Laura took stock. Her left shoulder burned, but she couldn't feel any blood up there. She hadn't felt any pain after she threw the punch, but now her right hand was beginning to throb badly. Then she heard a sound that got her attention. Mitzi was struggling for air. Had Laura's blow on the chin been hard enough to fracture the woman's jaw? Whether or not it did, the blow put Mitzi out deeply enough that her tongue had fallen backward, essentially choking her.

Although part of her wanted to let nature take its course, Laura realized she had to save Mitzi's life. It was difficult because of the pain in her right hand, but Laura rolled the unconscious woman onto her stomach and turned her head to the side. Almost immediately, the harsh, brassy croak of Mitzi struggling to take in air settled down to the stridor of a snorer. That took care of her airway.

A hand in front of Mitzi's face showed Laura the woman was breathing on her own. When Laura put her good left hand on Mitzi's neck, the carotid pulse was strong. She'd taken care of airway, breathing, and circulation. Now Laura needed to get some help.

Still using her left hand, Laura picked up the phone and held the receiver against her shoulder as she tapped in 9-1-1. She told the operator she needed the police immediately at her address. "A woman came into my house and shot at me. I think I've knocked her out, but I may still be in danger. Get someone here. Hurry!" Laura hung up while the operator was still talking because she thought she saw Mitzi move. She hadn't given an address, but because it was a landline, she knew the operator should be able to pinpoint the location.

Mitzi stirred briefly. Laura didn't want to use the gun, but knew it was the best way to be certain her prisoner didn't get up and rush her again. She picked it up with her left hand and pointed it at Mitzi, her finger outside the trigger guard. *I'm not sure I can shoot her, but if I have to, I will.* Then Mitzi slumped back to the floor and began to snore once more.

Officer Terrance Briggs recognized the house as soon as he pulled his car to a stop outside it. He left the driver's door open as he exited the car, the headlights and rotating strobe lights still on. Should he wait for backup? He shook his head. *They're on their way, but I can't wait.*

At the front door, he drew his service weapon. With the pistol in his right hand, he stood to the side of the door and pounded with his left fist. "Police. Open up."

A woman's voice from inside called, "It's unlocked. Come in."

There was nothing in the front hall, but he could see someone standing in the living room. He approached cautiously. You never knew what you were going to find when answering a "shots fired" call. What he saw, as he entered the living room, was one woman on her stomach on the floor, another standing over her with a pistol in her left hand.

"Ma'am, put the gun down and step away."

The woman complied. She turned toward him, and he recognized her.

"You're Dr. Morris," he said. "I saw you when I was here before."

The woman nodded. "Yes. Thank you for coming so quickly."

Briggs didn't lower his weapon but kept it pointing halfway between the woman on the floor and the one talking with him now.

"We got a call about shots fired," he said.

Dr. Morris pointed to the woman lying on the floor, now moaning a bit and apparently starting to wake up. "Yes, there were shots fired here—and she's the one who fired them."

Late that evening, when Laura called Robert to fill him in on developments, Claudia answered the phone.

"Robert isn't here, but he should be back in a few minutes. Can I give him a message?"

"Tell him the police have arrested Fay Autrey for killing Aunt Ina and hiding her body in a freezer. They're looking for Zack, except he wasn't really Zack. And then a woman tried to kill me, but I knocked her out—and now I have a painful right hand."

"Whoa, I think we're going to need more details than that." There was a brief pause. "Why don't we drive over and you can tell us all about it?"

Laura wondered what had caused Claudia to suggest they come over. She'd like to attribute it to a change of heart, but Laura figured there was more to it than that. The most likely explanation was that Claudia, now that the mystery of their aunt's death appeared to be solved, was curious about whether the police had dug deeply enough into her past to learn her secret. Maybe this was the time to put all the cards on the table and let Claudia know that she was an accepted member of the family, despite her past.

Despite Laura's objection that she was fine, Carter insisted on making the coffee. Then he pulled a coffee cake from the freezer and defrosted it. "You take care of that hand," he told Laura. "Tomorrow, we'll get it X-rayed."

The coffee was ready, and the cake stood next to the cups on the kitchen table when Robert and Claudia arrived. Carter carried it all into the living room.

Despite the metal splint and elastic bandage immobilizing Laura's right hand, she insisted on serving everyone herself. Then she settled in beside Carter and began. "This all started, I suppose, when Fay Autrey told Aunt Ina she wanted some money for the help she'd given her."

By the time Laura had finished her explanation, with interjections and side remarks from Carter, everyone had drained their coffee cups, and only crumbs remained of the cake.

"Sounds as though this is finally over," Robert said. "You know, I got a bad vibe from the man claiming to be Zack. Turns out, I was right."

"Yes, you were," Laura said. "And as a result of the police investigation, we've located our long-lost brother. I plan to fly to Las Vegas next week after Aunt Ina's funeral to see him."

"Are you going to bring him back here?" Claudia asked.

"I suppose it depends on what he wants to do," Laura said. "But I'm going to make it clear to Zack that his sister and his brother would love to have him back in Hilton—especially since he's got his life turned around." She looked pointedly at her older brother.

"I . . . I think that would be fine," Robert said.

"You know, one thing a family does is forgive," Laura said. "For instance, when you and Claudia were married, Carter hired a private detective to do some checking. We found out some things that surprised us."

"Why were you surprised?" Robert said. "I told you that Claudia and I met at SMU while I was in law school there."

"I suppose you could have met on campus," Carter said. "But Claudia never took a course there. It's more likely you met her in the course of her employment—dancing at a lounge off Mockingbird Lane in Dallas."

Laura watched her brother and sister-in-law as Carter spoke. Claudia frowned. Robert maintained a poker face.

"Claudia, you're intelligent and attractive," Laura said. "If you and Robert are in love, I think it's great that you're married. You each provide the other with what's wanted and needed. And, so far as your background goes, that doesn't make any difference to us. There's no need for you to try to hide it. We already know, and we love you anyway."

Claudia didn't say anything—just let out a sigh, perhaps one of relief, and nodded. But that was enough to let Laura know the message had been received.

"Why didn't you tell me about the way Mitzi had been coming on to you?" Laura asked.

It was very late, but Laura hadn't run down yet. She and Carter were seated at their kitchen table with steaming mugs of hot chocolate in front of them. Laura reached down with her left hand and lifted her cup.

"You had enough on your plate," Carter said. "Besides, I thought it was just a passing phase. I had no idea she was this serious about it."

"What's going to happen to her?" Laura asked.

"Depends on the evidence. The final decision is up to the authorities. They could charge her with anything from menacing to attempted murder. But I really think she needs some psychiatric help, and I hope that's what she gets. Her divorce hit her hard, then her ex-husband remarried, which was probably the thing that made her snap."

"Did the police find Zack—or Bud, I guess I should call him?"

"Patrolman Briggs talked with Sergeant Fuller before he left here earlier this evening, and the police had already picked up Bud. He was about thirty miles away, on his way out of town in your car, when they stopped him. We'll probably have to identify the fake Zack for them so they can press charges against him, but tomorrow is soon enough for that. And you should have your car back soon."

"So, I guess that's it," Laura said. "Except for one thing."

"Do you want to head for the ER and get that hand X-rayed tonight? If it's broken—"

"No, that's not what I wanted to talk about," Laura said.

"You mean the funeral for your aunt? Or the trip to Las Vegas to reunite with the real Zack? You can work on those tomorrow too."

"No, those can wait," Laura said. "This is about you and me."

"I don't understand," Carter said.

"When she was talking about why she was better qualified than me to be your wife, Mitzi called me barren. And I guess we both thought I was. But apparently we were all wrong." She gave Carter a weak smile. "I wanted to wait until I was certain, but I repeated the test, and it came up positive again."

Carter looked puzzled. "What are you saying?"

"Well, it's not the way we'd planned it. It's sort of a surprise. But even if we both are in our midthirties, I think it will be okay—especially if I retire from my practice to become a full-time wife and mother."

"You mean—?"

"Yes," Laura said. "You're going to be a daddy."

They stood and embraced each other. Out of the corner of her eye, Laura noticed one of the mugs turned on its side, spilling chocolate onto the kitchen table. But she didn't care.

The End

ACKNOWLEDGEMENTS

As is always the case with books, no matter the length and complexity of the manuscript, a number of people besides the author are involved in the work. In my case, I owe my thanks to five talented women: Rachelle Gardner, Kay Mabry, Susanne Lakin, Dineen Miller, and Virginia Smith. Without their help, this novella would never have been published.

DR. MABRY'S LATEST RELEASE

The latest full-length novel by Dr. Richard Mabry, *Miracle Drug*, was released on September 15, 2015. Here's a sample:

Tears formed in Rachel Moore's eyes as she stood on the tarmac of El Dorado airport in Bogotá, Colombia, watching the special metal coffin holding the earthly remains of Dr. Ben Lambert disappear into the cargo hold of the private jet. *Dr. Lambert, I'm so sorry. I wish I could have done more.*

An older man, the silver waves of his hair blowing slightly in the wind, stood beside her. As though he could read her thoughts, he said, "Don't beat yourself up, Rachel. No one could have predicted this. And you and the others did everything humanly possible. Ben was probably already dead when you found him." Then David W. Madison, immediate past President of the United States, put his arm gently around her shoulders and hugged her.

"I guess I know that," she said. "But no one expected it. I mean, we all had physicals along with our immunizations before leaving, and he told me he was in tip-top shape for a man of over sixty. Then, when we were eating lunch at the church, he was in the bathroom..."

"I know. It's a shock. Ben Lambert was an old friend. We grew up together. And now he's gone." Madison took his arm away and looked down at the nurse. "You know you don't have to be the one to accompany his body back to Dallas. One of the other members of the party could do it."

"No, I think I need this to achieve some closure. You'll be coming back in a couple more days, and if there's a medical problem after I leave, you still have Dr. Dietz and Linda Gaston."

The door to the cargo hold closed with a thud, and Rachel shivered despite the tropic heat. She lifted her carry-on bag and started to turn away, but Madison stopped her.

"Ben must have sensed something like this might happen, because before we left he spoke to me about another physician he thought should take care of me if he couldn't." Madison hesitated. "I think you know him. Matter of fact, I imagine he's the one meeting you at the airport after you land."

"You mean Josh?"

"Please tell Dr. Pearson I need to see him as soon as I return."

You can order *Miracle Drug* or any other book by Dr. Mabry via Amazon.com or your favorite bookseller.

Made in the USA
Middletown, DE
30 August 2024